INSTRUMENT OF DEATH . . .

It was painted in that invisible, midnight black, and as Chiun brought it back, Remo thought how eerie it was that even close up, he could see only the silhouette of the gadget. All the light that hit the center of the object was totally absorbed and reflected nothing to the eye.

"What is it, Chiun?"

"I believe it is your skull-crusher," Chiun said.

"Where'd you get it?"

"It was supposed to have made mush out of your worthless head, thereby making the outside identical to the inside," Chiun said.

"What do you mean?" Remo asked.

"Our invisible man had this around your head when I took it from him," Chiun said.

"And that's why you let him go? You were busy saving my life?"

"Actually, that was not on my mind," Chiun said. "I just thought this might be a valuable invention and worth saving for the world. Unlike some things, which are not worth saving at all."

"Little Father," said Remo.

"Yes."

"Thank you."

"You're welcome. You tell Smith that the invisible man got away."

THE DESTROYER SERIES:

#1 CREATED, THE DESTROYER
#2 DEATH CHECK
#3 CHINESE PUZZLE
#4 MAFIA FIX
#5 DR. QUAKE
#6 DEATH THERAPY
#7 UNION BUST
#8 SUMMIT CHASE
#9 MURDERER'S SHIELD
#10 TERROR SQUAD
#11 KILL OR CURE
#12 SLAVE SAFARI
#13 ACID ROCK
#14 JUDGMENT DAY
#15 MURDER WARD
#16 OIL SLICK
#17 LAST WAR DANCE
#18 FUNNY MONEY
#19 HOLY TERROR
#20 ASSASSIN'S PLAY-OFF
#21 DEADLY SEEDS
#22 BRAIN DRAIN
#23 CHILD'S PLAY
#24 KING'S CURSE
#25 SWEET DREAMS
#26 IN ENEMY HANDS
#27 THE LAST TEMPLE
#28 SHIP OF DEATH
#29 THE FINAL DEATH
#30 MUGGER BLOOD
#31 THE HEAD MEN
#32 KILLER CHROMOSOMES
#33 VOODOO DIE
#34 CHAINED REACTION
#35 LAST CALL
#36 POWER PLAY
#37 BOTTOM LINE
#38 BAY CITY BLAST
#39 MISSING LINK
#40 DANGEROUS GAMES
#41 FIRING LINE
#42 TIMBER LINE
#43 MIDNIGHT MAN

The Destroyer #43

Warren Murphy

MIDNIGHT MAN

PINNACLE BOOKS   LOS ANGELES

THE DESTROYER #43: MIDNIGHT MAN

Copyright © 1981 by Richard Sapir and Warren Murphy

An original Pinnacle Books edition, published for the first time anywhere.

First printing, February 1981

ISBN: 0-523-40717-3

Cover illustration by Hector Garrido

Printed in the United States of America

PINNACLE BOOKS, INC.
2029 Century Park East
Los Angeles, California 90067

For Trace, whom I never keep up late, and for the
House of Sinanju, P.O. Box 1454,
Secaucus, NJ 07094.

CHAPTER ONE

What Elmo Wimpler really wanted to invent was a dry cereal that tasted like ham and eggs. Or pancakes. Or all those other things he couldn't afford and didn't know how to cook.

But he didn't know how to do it, so he was stuck with dry cereal. One day cornflakes, then crisped rice, then that fruity stuff, then that chocolaty stuff. It was funny, he thought. If they could make a cereal taste like chocolate without putting any chocolate in it, why couldn't they make one that tasted like ham and eggs? Or Belgian waffles—with strawberries and whipped cream? Chipped beef on toast?

Why not? Maybe he'd work on that. But only when he was finished with the invention that occupied his mind right now.

Today, Elmo Wimpler had no idea what cereal he was eating. He had just grabbed the box, poured some into a bowl, drowned it with a weak mixture of powdered milk and water, and started eating. After a while they all tasted alike.

As he ate, he read his cyber-psychomatics book, which promised to teach him how to become a stronger-willed person.

Today, his heart wasn't into cyber-psychomatics, so he snapped the paperback closed and took another book from its spot on the kitchen table: *How to Be Pushy*.

1

He read two paragraphs and sighed. He just couldn't be pushy. He was too small, too mild-mannered. What would he do if he tried to be pushy and somebody pushed him back?

He closed the book and looked out the dirt-shaded window of the small kitchen. He'd like to try it, though. Just once. Maybe try being pushy with his big-mouth next-door neighbor, the no-talent jock. Just once, he'd like to put the big slob in his place, then make him watch while Elmo put himself right square into Mrs. No-Talent Jock's place. Despite that teased hair and that loud mouth, she was the creature of his dreams and his fantasies, and he would like to give it to her good.

He brought himself back to reality, which was his soggy bowl of cereal. He dumped it into the sink. Today, he felt as if he was getting near a breakthrough with his new invention.

Maybe when it was done. When he was acclaimed and rich and powerful. Maybe then, he'd show Mrs. Jock that men weren't measured by muscles alone.

Elmo Wimpler ran the water until all traces of the cereal had disappeared down the drain. Then he wiped the bowl once with a paper towel and put it on the drainboard. He started to walk back to his bedroom to change from his ratty bathrobe into his equally ratty clothes, but the impulse was too strong. He went back into the kitchen and got the book on being pushy. He read it while he walked down the hall. He bumped his ankle painfully against a cardboard box that was stuck against the wall. He tripped over his cat, who was lying majestically directly in the middle of the hallway. The cat

2

snarled, lashed out at Wimpler with his claws, and left gouge marks along the top of the man's foot. Wimpler apologized to his cat.

Elmo dressed quickly, hoping that he could make it to his garage workshop without running into his loud-mouthed neighbor, Curt, or his sexy, noisy wife, Phyllis. He didn't feel like dealing with them today, not when he was so close to a breakthrough.

He left his house by the rear door and walked quickly toward his garage. Too late. He heard a high-pitched woman's voice yell, "Hey, Curt. Look at the wimp. He's tryin' to sneak into his garage without us seeing him."

Damn.

Ignore them.

"Hey, wimp!" Curt yelled. "That light from your goddamned garage is still keeping us awake. You had better do something about it, you hear?"

Elmo looked up. He still didn't see them. He knew the light from his garage didn't bother them because there was no light from his garage. He had covered all the windows with heavy black plastic so no light would leak through. But he knew that would not satisfy Curt, and he was just tired of explaining.

"I'll work on it, Curt," he said. "I'm sorry."

"He's sorry, he says," Phyllis said. "Make him really sorry, Curt. Punch him out."

"Yeah. Maybe I should. And listen, that damned radio of yours, you're playing it too loud at night. How'd you like me to stuff it down your throat?"

Curt came around the corner of Elmo Wimpler's garage, six-foot-three, bulging biceps, bulging beer belly. He had steel-wool hair and a sneering mouth.

3

Behind him was Phyllis. She had teased blonde hair and also wore a sneer, but below the sneer, she wore a halter top over full breasts and a pair of skimpy, cutoff jeans that showed her ripe, round thighs. Elmo often saw her out his kitchen window while she was gardening, bent over, as if trying to show him her round, little bottom.

He thought about telling Curt that he didn't have a radio, that the only musical sound Curt might hear coming from the garage would be Elmo humming. But why bother?

"I'll try to keep it down, Curt," he told the big man, who blocked his way to the garage.

" 'I'll try to keep it down, Curt,' " Phyllis mimicked nastily. "He makes me sick. Belt him."

"He ain't worth it," Curt said, hitching up his pants, which immediately started their inevitable slide down his burgeoning belly.

"Go ahead, Curt, punch him out. Punch out his pissy little face."

Curt turned to tell Phyllis how he didn't want to dirty his hands on wimpy garbage, and Elmo took the opportunity to slip past the big man and into his garage. He shut and locked the door behind him. Suddenly he felt relief, but it lasted only a few seconds.

"I'll be waiting for you when you come out of there, wimp," Curt yelled. His voice, next to the garage door, sounded as if it might splinter the wood.

Elmo Wimpler put his neighbors out of his mind. He would be in his garage until long after they had gone to sleep. Here, there was peace. Here, where he was surrounded by his inventions, the works of

4

his life, which would someday bring him the fame and fortune he deserved.

But even as he thought it, he doubted himself. It had been so many years, and now the small estate that his parents had left him when they died was shrinking fast. He would have to make something commercial pretty soon.

He walked to the front of the garage to turn on the overhead light. He bumped his left knee on his car. Funny, he thought, that he hadn't seen it.

He reached out with his hands. He could feel the car, the hood, the fender, the windshield wipers. But he couldn't see it. All he could see was the dark, car-shaped silhouette in the dimness of his garage. But he couldn't see the car.

His heart beat a little faster, and he walked quickly to the light string, pulled it, and turned around. He almost yelled. The paint had worked.

In the harsh light overhead, the car was a deep black silhouette. But none of its features was visible.

It had worked! This time, he did yell. Let Curt scream. Who cared? Elmo Wimpler was on his way.

He had been testing paints, trying to invent a paint for cars that would defy rust and never need waxing. He had stumbled onto something better. He had mixed a black enamel with a special metallic formula. The paint appeared to be smooth, but under a microscope, the metallic compound was a field of pits and valleys. Light hitting the surface would not reflect back to a viewer's eye but would bounce back and forth inside the paint, from peak to peak. Unable to reflect light, anything coated with that paint would be totally black—100 percent black—and would be visible only in silhouette against something lighter. But none of its details could be made out. It was an invisible paint.

He touched the grill of the old car and felt the ripples and grooves of the once shiny metal. He took his hand away and leaned back. The grill was not visible.

He felt his heart pounding inside his chest. This was it. His big chance. No more dry cereal. No more living next door to Mr. and Mrs. Jock. No more trying to make do with old, worn-out equipment. No more working in a garage.

The invisible paint was his passport to a new life.

An hour later, he had his new paint compound in a spray can. Ignoring the hoots and calls of Curt and his wife, he walked quickly back into his house and called the FOI telephone number he had seen in a magazine—Friends of Inventors—a commercial group that would help him patent and sell his new paint.

The secretary told him that there was one opening later that afternoon, and he could make it if he hurried. The evaluation fee, payable in advance to FOI, was $500. Cash.

Elmo Wimpler dressed in his one suit, put his can of spray paint in a paper bag, and walked to the neighborhood bank. He had exactly $504 in his checking account, and he withdrew $502. Enough for the fee and bus fare both ways to FOI.

The pretty receptionist at FOI headquarters in New York City looked at him strangely as he arrived, clutching his paper bag under his arm.

"You have the five hundred dollars?" she asked. "Mister . . . Mister . . . Wimple," she said, glancing at a sheet on her desk.

6

"Wimpler," he corrected. He counted out the bills from his wallet, going slowly so he could look at her big, sweater-clad bosom. She smiled at him, a professional bored smile. When he gave her the money, she counted it, put it into her desk drawer, and announced into the intercom, "Mister Wimple is here."

"Wimpler," Elmo corrected.

"Send him in," a voice crackled over the speaker. She nodded him toward the door.

Inside the room, three men sat at a long table. They watched carefully as Wimpler approached them.

He placed the paper bag on the table, cleared his throat, and said, "I am Elmo Wimpler." He started to go on, but one of the men interrupted.

"Yeah, yeah, okay, guy, we're the panel you have to show your stuff to. We make all the decisions on inventions and like that. Show us what you got, 'cause we ain't got all day."

"Very well."

Wimpler opened the bag and took out a piece of black cloth, a small vase, and the spray can of paint.

He draped the black curtain over a small picture that hung from the wall.

"C'mon, pal, speed it up," the same man told him. "You're not setting a stage, you know. We've got a lot of other geniuses to see, so don't be wasting our time."

Elmo adjusted the black cloth so it hung smoothly.

"Jesus Christ, what is this guy, an interior decorator?" one of the other men said.

Wimpler ignored them. When they saw what his

7

invention did, then they'd know he was no crackpot, there to waste their time and his money.

He moved a small table over in front of the painting and set the white vase on the table. It was an ornately carved, cheap, little, milk-glass vase.

Without paying any attention to the three men, he sprayed the white vase with his spray can of black paint. He turned to look at the three members of the panel with a smug look on his face.

They looked at him as if he were from another planet.

"So, you got a black vase?" one of them said. "And it used to be white."

"Watch. It'll dry quickly," Elmo said. He turned to watch himself. The paint was drying before his eyes, and as it did, the definition of the vase seemed to vanish. And then the paint was dried, and the vase was invisible against the black cloth background.

"Invisible," Elmo said with a small, proud smile.

"What the hell good is an invisible vase?" one of the men asked. "Why would anyone want an invisible vase?"

The three men began to chuckle and dig elbows into each other. Elmo Wimpler couldn't believe what he was seeing and hearing. Were they blind? Didn't they realize what a great invention this was?

"It's invisible," he said. "That's invisible paint. Don't you understand? Anything you paint that color won't reflect any light. In the dark or against a black background, it'd be invisible. Against a lighter background, you'd only be able to see its silhouette. You wouldn't be able to make out any of its details."

"Big deal," one of the men said. "Suppose you painted a car that color?" another asked. To Wimpler, the three men were interchangeable, like triplets. "I mean, you never remember where you park it now, but if you couldn't see it, that'd make it even worse. People would keep backing into you. At night, like I mean, who wants a car you can't see?"

They began to laugh again and Elmo closed his eyes, trying to remember some necessary paragraphs from *How to Be Pushy*. Fight back, he told himself. Fight back. But he could not utter a single word in his own defense. He watched them and listened helplessly to their inane chatter.

"You still got that Cadillac, Ernie?" one man asked another.

"Yeah, but I may be selling it."

"Why? That car's beautiful."

"Yeah, but it sucks up gas like a pack of Tums. Who needs that?"

"I could use it. Have to change the color though," the first man said. Suddenly all three seemed to remember Wimpler.

"You got anything in mauve?" asked the one who was thinking about buying Ernie's Cadillac. "Mauve is going to be a hot color this year. A lot of mauve. Maybe if you could do something in mauve."

"Maybe for kids," Ernie suggested. "Maybe they might want to make things invisible, like if they don't want their folks to find them. I mean, maybe if you sprayed this on a joint of marijuana . . . would it change the flavor? What does this paint taste like?"

"Taste?" asked Wimpler helplessly. He shook his head, blinking his eyes hard.

9

"Yeah, you know, if it tastes like shit, it'd make the grass taste like shit and nobody'd want it. But if it doesn't change the taste, then maybe somebody might want invisible marijuana."

"I think we're agreed," the third man said, "that it is not prudent to represent this item in its present form."

All three nodded toward Elmo.

"Work on the taste," Ernie suggested.

"And the color," the second man said.

"Mauve," said the third man. "Work on mauve. A hot color this year."

"That's it?" Elmo finally sputtered. "You talk about cars, you talk about mauve, you give me two minutes, and you say good-bye?"

"That's it," the team leader said. "It's impractical in its present form, Mr. Wimple."

"Wimpler."

"Yes, Mister Wimper. I'm afraid it's impractical. Now, if you had something to do with a barbecue, maybe. People are into barbecues again with inflation running rampant. But not an invisible barbecue. There's no market for that."

"Try mauve," another man suggested.

"I paid you five hundred dollars," Wimpler shouted.

"Nonrefundable," Ernie snapped. "You understood that when you came in. Nonrefundable. Now, we have other people to see, Mister Simple, so if you're finished? . . . We have a man to see about a back scratcher that's supposed to revolutionize the art of scratching your back."

"That sounds interesting," said one of the other

men. The third man agreed but suggested it might sell best in mauve.

A back scratcher.

Elmo Wimpler packed up his curtain, his invisible black vase, and his spray can and left, shaking his head. On the way out, he didn't even notice the receptionist's forty-inch chest. She was busy talking to a man who was offering to demonstrate how useful his back scratcher would be for front scratching too.

By the time he got home, Elmo had decided to finance himself in marketing his invisible spray paint. Thank God he had money—a little money—still left in stocks and savings. He called the banker who was the trustee for his parents' estate and asked him how much money was left.

"Nothing," the man answered.

"Nothing?" Elmo said. "How can that be? There's a mistake." *Please let there be a mistake,* he thought.

"I'm sorry, Elmo, but I saw a chance to increase your holdings and made some investments."

"I didn't authorize any investments," Wimpler snapped.

"I know," said the banker, sounding huffy over the phone. "But I knew you wouldn't mind. So I put your money in gold."

"And gold dropped from eight hundred to six hundred an ounce. I should have something left."

"No," the banker explained patiently. "I bought on margin. The two-hundred-dollar drop wiped you out. Sorry about that."

"My house," said Wimpler. "I can mortgage it. What can I get?"

"Too late. You really should have called me last week. I mortgaged your house."

"Damn," snarled Wimpler.

"Well, if you let me know once in a while what's on your mind . . ." the banker said. "I can't read minds, you know. Anyway, if I can be of any more . . ."

Wimpler hung up.

He was broke.

Ruined.

And hungry.

But there was no food in the house. Nothing but dry cereal and powdered milk, and he gagged just thinking about it.

He fell into a chair, holding his head between his hands. What could he do now? He had no family, no friends to turn to for help. He could starve to death and no one would know. Here he had this great invention worth millions. Imagine all the things that could be made invisible. Tanks. Airplanes. An army. Policemen. Burglars.

Wait a minute.

He sat straight up in the chair and reran everything that had just gone through his head until he found the one he wanted.

Burglars.

Could he do it? Did he have the nerve?

Was anything worse than starving to death?

He began to walk to his bedroom, slowly at first, then with more determination. He tripped over his cat. The cat spat. Elmo Wimpler apologized.

From his closet he took an old shirt and slacks and his only other pair of shoes.

He hung them on the back of a door and began

to spray the clothing. He sprayed the shoes black and put them back into the dark closet. As the paint dried, the shoes disappeared.

He began to get excited at the prospect of playing the invisible man. He ran to the kitchen, again tripping over the cat. This time he did not apologize. From a plastic wrap and an old baseball cap, he fashioned a face screen with a thin slit he could see through. He took it back to the bedroom and sprayed the whole aparatus black.

He put on the costume, then drew the blinds and old drapes in the room. He stepped in front of the full length mirror on the back of his bedroom door in the dark room and there he was.

Or wasn't.

He was invisible.

He felt a thrill like he'd never felt before, not even when he was watching Phyllis' bottom as she gardened next door. He felt fantastic.

And scared.

CHAPTER TWO

His name was Remo and he feared nothing.

All men's fears were based on one thing alone—the fear of dying. It was what terrified an embezzler; afraid he might be found out, and afraid he would have to take his own life. It explained the terror of a child in the dark, or a grown-up hearing the sound of rats inside a wall. Every fear translated into the fear of dying.

And Remo no longer had that fear. He no longer worried about being killed, but only about whom he would kill and when.

He was an assassin, and knowing that he had power over life and death for others had given him a kind of peace he had never known before.

He felt that peace as he slipped into the hospital, strolled with a casual wave past a guard's desk, and nodded to a middle-aged nurse, who took one look at the slim, thick-wristed, dark-eyed man and wished that he belonged to her.

Remo whistled peacefully as he rode in the elevator up to the intensive care unit on the third floor and found a linen closet. Inside, a simple change of clothes made him an orderly.

He loaded his arms up with a pile of towels, walked into the intensive care ward and said to the young peppermint striper there, "How's it going tonight?"

The young woman took one look into his intense, dark eyes and felt the same shiver the nurse downstairs had felt.

"Quiet as a mouse," she said. "You're new here, aren't you?"

"Yup," he said. He leaned over her desk and, as he checked the list of patient names in the ward, breathed into her ear. "Show me around later?"

His hand touched her back and did something to her that made her squirm on the orange plastic seat cushion.

"Sure," she said, and then in case he had misunderstood her statement or its intensity, said again, "Sure. Sure."

"Swell," he said, removing his hand. "Meet you here later."

Still carrying his towels, he found the orderlies' lounge down the hall. Inside was a tall, dark-haired man, drinking coffee and studying a typewritten sheet. When Remo entered, he hurriedly put the sheet away, but Remo had already recognized it: it was the patient list from intensive care.

This was number one.

Remo poured himself some unwanted coffee. His nose rebelled at the smell and his brain at the thought of drinking a mud created from boiling burned beans. Then he sat across from the other orderly.

"You the man?" he asked.

"Huh?" the dark-haired man said, his eyes nearly watering behind his wire-rimmed glasses.

"You know what I mean. You running the pool?" Remo asked.

"What pool?"

"C'mon, pal," Remo said, "I've got to get back on duty. Who's on the list? Mrs. Grayson? What days you got left?"

The thin man blinked several times behind his glasses, then said slowly, "Twenty-first and twenty-fifth."

"Hell," Remo said. "She'll go before that but give me the twenty-first."

"It'll cost you fifty," the orderly said.

"Got it right here," Remo said, reaching into his pocket. But of course his cash was in the pocket of his black chinos, underneath the white hospital trousers he was wearing. So he drove his fingertips through the bottom of the empty pocket, ripping the fabric, then reached through the hole into his chino pocket and brought out a roll of bills.

As he pretended to count off fifty dollars, Remo said, "I've heard that some of you guys are pulling the plugs on these patients. That doesn't seem fair."

The thin orderly grinned. "Everybody's got the same chance. If Mrs. Grayson lives to your day, and you pull the plug on her and nobody notices and she conks, well, then you're the winner." He grinned. "It's simple. Everybody's got an equal chance to get the pool."

Remo held fifty dollars toward the man, who extended his hand for it.

"Ever wonder?" Remo said.

"Wonder what?"

"How it feels to get your own plug pulled?" The man looked up, and met Remo's eyes. Remo smiled, reached out and unplugged the orderly's windpipe.

Remo tossed the body into a coat closet, took the typewritten sheet from the man's shirt pocket and went back into the room. He sat at the table with the sheet flattened out before him.

Another orderly entered the room. He was a squat blond, whose bristled haircut made him look like a squared-off stack of hay.

"Where's Arnie?" he asked Remo.

"Gone," Remo said. He looked up from the list. "What day you got?"

"Nineteenth." The man poured himself a cup of coffee. "How much we collect so far?" he asked.

"Look for yourself," Remo said. He pushed the sheet across the table. The man reached for it and Remo said, "Arnie's dead."

"Dead? How . . ."

"I pulled his plug," Remo said. "Like this." The husky blond saw Remo's hand start to move, but he never saw it reach him, never saw the fingers flip out from the coiled fist, never felt them slap away at his throat, deftly removing his Adam's apple and windpipe with no more effort than if Remo had been flicking a sandfly from his wrist.

He put the blond in the same closet where he'd put Arnie and sat waiting for the third orderly. These three were the organizers; the rest of the bettors were just having some macabre fun. They were content to lose if the patients lived. So far as upstairs knew, none of them had anything to do with killing patients.

Arnie was the first. The second had been Billy according to his name tag. That left Jackie. The door opened and an orderly came in wearing the name tag of Jackie.

It was a woman.

Remo hadn't suspected that. But "Jackie" could

17

be male or female. He should have known that upstairs would forget to tell him about a minor point like that.

It didn't bother him. He had killed women before.

"Where's Arnie and Billy?" she asked.

"Dead," he said.

She was too busy looking into his eyes and smiling to hear him. She sat in the chair across from him. "When will they be back?"

She was pretty. Green eyes, auburn hair, good breasts, and a clean-well-washed smell.

"What are you doing with that sheet?" she asked, pointing to the paper in front of Remo.

"Arnie gave it to me," Remo said. "What day do you have?"

"Eighteenth," she said. "Tomorrow. Guess I'll have to pull a plug," she said with a smile. "What'd you say happened to Arnie and Billy?"

"Ask them yourself," Remo said. Her eyes widened as he unplugged her windpipe. Her eyes really were a pretty green.

He dumped her into the coat closet with the two men, and stood back to savor his handiwork.

"That's the lottery biz, sweethearts," he said and slammed the door.

He waved to the peppermint striper on his way out, dumped his whites into a laundry bin, waved to the older nurse at the front desk and left the hospital.

The terminal cases could now terminate on their own. It made Remo feel good.

But not for long.

He had other assignments that night.

18

CHAPTER THREE

Elmo Wimpler had been frightened of becoming a burglar but he was more frightened of starving to death, penniless, unknown, friendless.

He had waited until late night, and then had donned his black uniform. He turned out the lights over his front door, then stepped out into his yard.

He looked down at himself. He could barely see the outline of his feet and legs. He understood that he was slightly visible in silhouette because of the lights reflecting around the street. He would have to remember that he was most effective in pitch darkness.

He cut through backyards, behind houses, once passing only inches from a sleeping German shepherd who did not stir as Wimpler walked by. With each step, Elmo felt the power growing in him.

He knew what house he would hit. It was in the Park Slope section only a few blocks from his home. He had often walked by the house, a big brick and stucco English tudor design with a long, black Cadillac parked out front.

Elmo slipped around the back of the house and waited on the darkened porch, trying to calm his nerves and still the thumping of his heart. He might be invisible but his heart was making so much noise he could be heard a block away.

Finally, he tapped lightly on the doorbell and

moved off to the side. A few moments later, a young black woman dressed in a maid's uniform came to the door and looked out.

"Who's there?" he could hear her ask through the glass.

He held his breath. Finally, she opened the storm door and stepped out on the porch, holding the door open behind her. He slipped through the door as he heard her mutter, "Damn fool kids."

Inside, he moved quickly into a darkened corner and waited for the maid to come back inside. His heart was racing. Suddenly he was overcome by terror.

What if he was caught?

If the maid turned on a light, he would be as visible as if he had been dressed in neon.

In the future, he would have to plan his jobs more carefully.

But the maid walked by him without turning on a light. She went on and stepped into the living room.

"Who was that, Flo?" a man's voice asked.

Wimpler moved quietly along the hall, as he heard the maid say, "Just some kids, Mr. Mason."

"I hope they didn't wake Mrs. Mason."

As Wimpler reached the door, he peered in from the shadows. The man was getting up from the sofa. He was fortyish, well-fed, and prosperous looking. "I have to go out, Flora," the man said. "Don't wake Mrs. Mason."

"Yes sir. You'll be back soon?"

Mr. Mason put his hands around the maid's rump and pulled her to him. He kissed her heavily on the mouth. "Soon enough," he said. "Soon enough."

Flora giggled as Mason walked toward a coat

rack near the door. Wimpler slipped quickly upstairs. If they had jewels, they would probably be in the master bedroom.

Only one of the upstairs doors was closed. Waiting outside, Wimpler could hear the sound of soft breathing. He opened the door, stepped inside, and saw a figure on the bed. He caught his breath.

Mrs. Mason slept atop the covers, in the nude. She wasn't as full-figured as Phyllis, his next door neighbor, but she would do. She was in her thirties and well-kept, with large breasts and long slim legs.

Wimpler found himself starting to get excited, imagining the things he could do to her while she slept. And if she awoke and saw no one in the room, she would probably think she had been dreaming.

Some dream.

Wimpler almost laughed.

But first things first. With an effort, he turned away from the woman and began searching the room. He found what he was looking for in a top drawer of the dresser. A jewelry box was filled with necklaces and bracelets and rings. He took them all and put them in a small, cloth bag he had brought with him. Then he secreted the bag under his invisible clothing.

He turned back to the sleeping, nude form of Mrs. Mason.

But fear overcame his lust. It was time to leave. He reached down and playfully stroked one of Mrs. Mason's breasts. She smiled in her sleep. Then he whispered in her ear, "Your husband and your maid are making it, dear."

The smile slid off her face and Wimpler went quickly to the door and went down the stairs.

When he finally got back to his own house, he heaved a sigh of relief. He removed his black night suit and dumped his take out on the bed.

The diamonds sparkled and shone and he let them wash through his fingers as he played with them on the bed. How much, he wondered. Ten thousand? Twenty?

He'd find out tomorrow, when he went to 47th Street in Manhattan to sell them.

As he got off the subway at 47th Street and Avenue of the Americas, he was surprised to realize his heart was pounding again.

What if someone called the police?

He took a deep breath and walked into the first wholesale jeweler he saw.

"May I help you?" a clerk asked. Was that suspicion in the man's eyes, Wimpler wondered. He almost backed out, but then cleared his throat and said, "I want to . . . er . . . sell some jewelry. It was . . . my mother's. She's dead now."

"May I see it?"

Wimpler dumped the contents of his cloth bag on the counter. He could feel the sweat running in rivulets under his arms.

"Lovely pieces," the clerk said.

"Mmmmmm," said Wimpler, afraid to say more because his throat was so dry that he might not be able to get any words out.

The clerk looked at them for interminable seconds.

"I'll have to call the manager," he said.

"Why?" Wimpler sputtered out. "What's . . ."

"He has to appraise them," the clerk said with a suspicious smile. As Wimpler watched the man's retreating back, he knew what was going to happen. In the back room, the clerk was going to pick up a telephone and call the police. Inside of thirty seconds, the store would be surrounded.

Wimpler turned and ran from the store, racing down 47th Street to the subway station and down the steps.

He got off the subway at 42nd Street where he realized that he had left the jewels behind. So much for his buglary career.

He walked the streets. He passed six hot dog venders, eight pizza shops, two MacDonalds, a Burger King, Chinese take-out food shops, food stores by the dozen, noticed and counted only because he was starving.

He fished in his pocket. He had fifty cents. In New York, it wasn't even enough for a sidewalk hot dog. And besides, he wanted to go home. He went down to the subway platform, took the train back to Brooklyn, got off at Atlantic Avenue and walked down to the docks.

His father had always told him that a man should know when to cut his losses. That is what Wimpler had in mind. Life had been a loss for him, a total loss, and now he was going to cut those losses. He stood staring at the filthy water, wondering if he would have the nerve to throw himself in and end his misery. He walked along the dock, trying to build up his nerve, when suddenly he heard voices. For some reason, he darted behind a large packing crate and listened.

"He's got to be iced, Jack," he heard one man say. "There's no way around it. If Romeo testifies, we're all cooked."

"Yeah, sure," the other man said with disgust. "But try to do it with all that freaking, federal security around him."

"If he testifies . . ."

"Don't tell me what I know already, Tony. Shit. I offered this hit to everyone in town. Nobody wants to touch it. I think we're gonna have to put together a squad and go up there and take the whole place out."

"The man won't like that, Jack. Too much bad press. A lot of blood, a lot of bodies, a lot of reporters, and a lot of feds."

"You know another way?"

Suddenly, Elmo Wimpler knew that he was not going to take his own life. Suddenly, he knew that his days as a wimp were over. Suddenly, he felt power. Power over life and death.

He took a deep breath and stepped out into the view of the two men.

"What? the . . . ?" one yelled.

"Who are you?" the other snarled.

"The answer to your problem," Wimpler said with confidence and a sureness he had never felt before. "Whoever it is you want iced, I can do it."

"Wha . . . ?" said Jack.

"You?" Tony asked, unbelievingly. Elmo knew what they were thinking: that he was a clown. He had been called all those names: clown, nerd, wimp. But he wasn't. Not any more. What he was now was the best hit man money could hire.

"Don't let appearances deceive you," he said. "I can do what you want done."

The two men looked at each other. Tony shrugged.

"What've we got to lose, Jack?" he finally said.

Jack sighed, then nodded. He looked at Wimpler. "How much?"

Elmo cleared his throat. He hadn't thought about money.

"Would a thousand dollars be too much?" he asked.

"You do the job, you get *ten* thousand dollars," Jack said.

"This person will be dead tomorrow night," Wimpler said. "Tell me who he is and where he is."

They told him. He was a big-time gangster, now a federal witness, testifying to save his own skin. He was being hidden out on a large, private estate in Westchester County, surrounded by cops, FBI agents, and who knew what else.

"Be here tomorrow night. Two A.M.," Wimpler said. "And bring the money."

"All right," said Jack.

"I need an advance," said Wimpler.

"How much?" Jack asked, reaching into his pocket.

All Wimpler could think of was a steak dinner. He decided to think big. "Twenty dollars," he said.

Jack leafed through the hundred dollar bills in his roll until he found a lone twenty and handed it over.

"Thank you. Tomorrow night. Two A.M.," Wimpler said.

"Sure, pal," Jack said. Elmo turned and walked away. He stopped at the first cheap steak place he saw, ordered two steak dinners and devoured them both. With his change, he took a cab home.

He hurried to his garage. He had his first contract but how would he carry it out? What would he use to kill his victim?

He searched through his garage, overturning useless inventions until he found the item he wanted.

Wimpler had worked it out as a revolutionary new nutcracker, but it hadn't sold. It was a small hand-held compressor. After fitting it with a long slide arm that would allow it to hold something bigger than walnuts, Elmo tried it out on an old bowling ball in the garage. The compressor's arms reached around the ball, and when he pressed the trigger, the two arms closed together with a hiss. The bowling ball broke up into hundreds of pieces that fell to the floor.

Done. All he would have to do would be to spray paint it, and the invisible man would have his invisible weapon.

And then he went to sleep. The first good night's sleep he had had in months.

The next morning, he cleaned the black paint from the windshield and windows of his old car parked in the garage. Then he quickly painted over the invisible, black paint with a light-blue, spray enamel, letting the paint run in drippy, gooey masses, not caring how the paint job looked, but just wanting to make the car visible again, presentable for riding around the street.

Then he drove up to White Plains and rode past the large estate where the federal witness was being held. In the gathering dusk, he could see guards stationed near the door of the house and lounging about on the lawn.

But for some reason, he was no longer afraid.

Wimpler drove around for a while and when it

was fully dark, he parked about a half-mile from the estate. Inside the auto, he changed into his invisible clothing, treated with what he now didn't mind calling WIMP—Wimpler's Invisible Metallic Paint.

The edge of the road was lined with trees and Elmo walked behind the trees in the dark, toward the estate.

He moved through the shadows toward the house. Once he passed within two feet of a guard who was looking right at him but didn't see him. Wimpler was tempted to play games, to tap one on the shoulder or to whisper in one's ear, but he decided to stick to business.

It was all business. There was no panic, no fear. Just a cold sense that this was what he had been put on earth to do. To kill.

He entered the house through a side French door. Two men were in the darkness of the room, but they did not see him.

"The door's open," one said.

"Must have been the wind," the other said, and got up to close the door.

Wimpler scouted through the house, hiding in shadows, listening to conversations. The police, it seemed, liked the federal witness no better than the mob did. Everybody seemed to wish someone would just blow him away and save everybody a lot of trouble.

Elmo Wimpler was going to save them a lot of trouble.

He found his victim in an upstairs bedroom, sitting in a chair, watching television in the darkened room. Anybody who watched reruns of "Gilligan's Island" deserved to die, Elmo thought.

He quietly walked up behind the man, opened up the arms of his compressor device, quickly clapped it to both sides of the man's head, and before the man could move, depressed the trigger.

There was a sharp hiss, the crack of bones, and a man with a head in pieces.

Wimpler went out through a window and climbed carefully down a trellis to the dark side of the house. Without looking back, he cut across the field, passing near guards, heading for his car parked down the street. He had to resist the urge to shout exultantly. He had done it. He had done it.

He did not change from his WIMP invisible outfit, but merely took off the hood for his drive back to Brooklyn.

He reached the docks early, but so had Jack and Tony, and standing in the shadows, Wimpler heard their conversation.

"The guy did it, Tony. He did it. I heard it on the radio."

"It's too bad we have to ice him, Jack. He's got style."

"I know. But if the man found out we farmed this out to an amateur . . . forget it, baby."

Elmo watched as each checked his gun, then slid it back into its shoulder holster.

"You gentlemen are not very honest," he said.

Jack's head snapped around. He looked questioningly into the dark, seeing nothing.

"Who said that?" Tony demanded.

"I did," Wimpler said. As Tony reached for his gun, Wimpler slid the invisible compressor over the man's head. A moment later, Tony was dead.

Jack threw up on what was left of his body.

"You can't see me, Jack, but I can see you," Wimpler said.

"What do you want?" Jack gasped.

"My money, Jack. That's what I want."

"Ten grand."

"Make it twenty for my extra trouble. Go and get it. And bring it here. And if you try anything funny, you'll join your friend."

Pale and shaking, Jack nodded. Wimpler watched him walk to his car, talking to himself. He knew the man would be back.

He was, in less than half an hour, holding twenty thousand dollars in cash in his hand. He saw it plucked from his hand, hanging in the air, seemingly of its own power. But before he had a chance to marvel too long, he joined his friend Tony in death.

As he left the dock on Atlantic Avenue, Wimpler thought that not only were Jack and Tony dead. There was another body back on that dock too.

The wimp was dead.

CHAPTER FOUR

Upstairs was getting less and less reasonable, Remo thought, as he drove up toward White Plains.

Getting rid of three hospital orderlies all at once was no big deal, but what was the hurry about then having to race over and check the security on some federal witness? It couldn't wait until tomorrow?

Remo found the address in White Plains and turned his rented Ford into the driveway, expecting to be stopped by guards.

There were no guards.

He drove up the long driveway to the house and was not challenged once. Several men milled about on the front steps. They looked up as Remo walked toward them.

"Anybody want to see my ID?" Remo asked.

"What for?" one man asked. He was seated on the top step, smoking a cigarette.

"Security," Remo said.

"What security? There's nothing to secure, nothing to guard." Then, as if suddenly curious, the man asked, "Who are you anyway, pal?"

"I was sent to check on your security," Remo said. "I have to tell you, so far you're a double D-minus."

"Our client won't mind anymore," the man said. The other men on the steps chuckled.

Remo went inside and followed the noise upstairs, where he found a gang of federal officers and local police milling around the front bedroom.

On the floor were pieces of the federal witness's head. His body was two feet away from the pieces.

"You guys couldn't guard a parked car," Remo growled, wheeled around, and walked toward the door of the room. It was all he needed, to listen to Upstairs bitching about the dead witness.

There had been ten years of listening to Upstairs bitch. Ever since Remo Williams, a young Newark policeman, was framed for a murder he didn't commit, sent to an electric chair that didn't work, and signed up to work for CURE, a secret agency that didn't exist. CURE was meant to fight criminals without having to worry about the constitutional restrictions against unfair tactics that seemed to tie the hands of every police department in the country. Remo was to be CURE's enforcement arm.

His boss was Dr. Harold W. Smith, the only director CURE had ever had, a man so rigid and rockhard, that even now, after ten years, Remo still had no idea what was on the man's mind at any time.

It had been ten years of work and ten years of training. Training at the hands of an eighty-year-old Korean, Chiun, the latest Master of the House of Sinanju, an ages-old house of assassins from Korea. Remo had taken the training, and he had learned it was more than training. It had not so much changed what he could do. It had changed what he was. And in that changing, it had given him the power to be more than man. And still, sometimes, he would have traded it all for a woman and children and a place to live that wasn't a hotel room.

* * *

Chiun's hands were bridged in front of his eyes, fingertip to fingertip and, as Remo entered the hotel room the ancient Korean did not look up. His golden kimono, draped around his slight body, looked like an elegant pile of laundry on the floor.

"Have you made it possible for old people to die in peace?" he asked.

"Yes," Remo said. "There was a surprise."

"What was that?" Chiun said, still studying his fingertips.

"The leader was a woman."

"And she was young and pretty," Chiun said.

"Yes."

"And this surprises you?"

"Well, I figured some fat guy with a beer belly and a bookie bill he couldn't pay."

Chiun lowered his hands, shook his head, and looked toward Remo. "You never learn," he said. "All women are killers, and the young, pretty ones are the worst because they think their beauty is their license to kill. You taught her respect for her elders?"

"I showed them what it was like to have their plugs pulled," Remo said.

"Isn't it ironic," Chiun said, "that someone like you, the most disrespectful of men, should be dispatched to teach someone else respect for their elders?"

"I respect you, Chiun. Honest."

"How easily the lies spring to your lips," Chiun said. "Like the dew suddenly appearing on the morning lily."

32

"All right, you're on the snot. Who got you there? Smitty called, right?"

Chiun nodded slowly. "Yes. The Emperor called. He seemed very upset with you. And well he should be. He is your Emperor, Remo, and yet you do nothing he tells you."

"I did everything tonight he told me to do."

"Yes? And at the Plains of White?"

"Plains of White?" Remo said aloud. "Plains . . . White Plains, right. He wanted me to look at the security for a federal witness."

"And?"

"And there was a problem," Remo said. "The witness was dead when I got there."

"The Emperor seems to think you have gone mad. He lectured me on telling you to keep your instructions straight. Are you sure you didn't . . . ?"

"Dead when I got there, Chiun," insisted Remo. "Some security. Somebody goofed good."

"Probably somebody young," Chiun said.

When Remo and Chiun arrived at the Folcroft Sanitarium in Rye, New York, only fifteen minutes from their hotel room, Dr. Harold W. Smith was standing in his office, his hands clasped behind his back, staring out the one-way glass at the darkness of Long Island Sound. Even from behind, without seeing Smith's face, Remo could tell that the CURE director was upset.

"What's the matter, Smitty? Somebody in the kitchen take an extra helping of strawberries?"

Remo saw Smith's hands clench. He stood in front of Smith's desk. Chiun sat in a hardbacked chair alongside the desk.

Smith finally wheeled around. "I can't believe you," Smith snapped.

"What the hell'd I do this time?" Remo asked.

"How could you be so . . . so . . . ?" Smith struggled.

"Idiotic," Chiun offered.

Smith shook his head. "So . . ."

"Dopey," suggested Chiun.

"So careless," Smith finally sputtered out.

"I liked dopey better," Chiun said.

"How could you get two assignments fouled up? I suppose you spent the night bodyguarding some homicidal hospital orderlies?"

Remo shook his head.

"An explanation," Smith said. "Is that too much to ask for? One that makes some sense? Two important assignments and you mix them up." Smith leaned on the back of his desk chair. "We've lost a very important federal witness now, because you couldn't keep assignments straight in your mind. Why in God's name did you kill Romeo?"

"Are you finished?" Remo asked.

"Show respect," Chiun scolded him. "This is your Emperor." He turned to Smith with a nod. "Continue, Emperor."

"I'm finished," Smith said. Both he and Chiun looked at Remo.

"I didn't kill Romeo," Remo said.

"No? Then who did? Chiun?" said Smith.

"Not me," Chiun said. "I have learned in many years that you only want me to remove those you want me to remove. I no longer try to guess who they are. Anyway, this was probably sloppy and you

34

know that an execution by a Master of Sinanju is a work of art. A thing of beauty. A . . ."

"Excuse me, Little Father," Remo interrupted, "but I don't think Smitty really suspects you, so please let me defend myself."

Chiun glared at Remo for the interruption but remained silent.

"Why do you think it was me?" Remo said.

"Who else? Who else could get to that house through two dozen guards and enough guard dogs for a breeding kennel. Who else could have crushed his skull into pieces? Pieces all over the room?"

"Well, first of all, it wasn't me. Second of all, those hospital people are dead. If they haven't reported it yet to the police, have them check the clothes closet in the orderlies' room on the third floor."

Smith paused, as if considering Remo's statements. He sat back down, made a phone call, spoke a few moments, and then hung up.

He stared at the receiver in his hand.

"They found the bodies in the hospital," he said.

"Am I off the hook?" Remo said.

"The telephone is off the hook," Chiun said. He pointed a long fingernail at the receiver and Smith hung it back up.

"If not you, who? Who else could have that kind of power?" Smith asked.

"We know it wasn't me. That's a start," Remo said.

"I never suspected you for a moment," Chiun said.

"I appreciate your faith, Little Father."

35

"Faith comes naturally to a great Master of Sinanju," Chiun said.

So does greed, thought Remo, remembering the shipload of gold that went to Chiun's village of Sinanju every year, as payment for training Remo. But he kept the observation to himself.

Inside Smith's desk, Remo could hear machinery whirring. Smith touched a button and a computer console lifted up from the desk. It flickered on and as Remo watched, Smith's face was bathed in a green glow as he read the information that the CURE computer was sending him.

Finally, he sighed, pressed another button and the console receded into the desk.

He looked at Remo. "Police in Brooklyn have found the bodies of two men on a pier there. They were killed the same way as the federal witness, Romeo."

"And now there are three," said Remo.

"And now there is trouble," Smith said. "There is some sort of strange power at work here. Capable of moving around without being seen. Capable of crushing a man's skull. And we better find out who it is."

"The two guys in Brooklyn?" Remo asked. "Anything there for a lead?"

"Just some drunk on the pier. He said he was sleeping behind boxes and he peeked out when he heard voices and he saw two men talking to a man who wasn't there. And the man he couldn't see was answering them."

"Two people. Three voices," Remo said. "One of them probably belonged to the drunk's pink elephant."

"Then we'd better find that pink elephant," Smith said caustically, "because he's got a way to crush people's skulls."

"Who were the victims in Brooklyn?" Remo asked.

"Two small-time hoods. But members of the Mafia family that had put out the contract on Romeo."

"You think they're connected?" Remo asked.

"It certainly seems that way," Smith said. "Three people with skulls shattered like walnut shells. It's no coincidence."

"Good," Remo said. "Let all the gang guys get killed off. It saves us work."

"We can't assume that that's what is going on," Smith said.

"Of course, we cannot assume that," Chiun chided Remo. "What a dopey assumption." He looked pleased that he had finally been able to slip "dopey" into the conversation.

Smith nodded. "Considering our present situation—the nation's situation—we can't afford to make any assumptions at all."

"What situation?" Remo asked suspiciously.

"The presence of the former Emir of Bislami."

"Oh, him," Remo said.

"He comes from a good family," Chiun said. "Bislami was always one of the favorites of our house. Did I ever tell you about the time during the year of the great wind when . . . ?"

Smith interrupted and was rewarded with a glare. "The new rulers of Bislami have placed a ten-million-dollar price tag on his head."

"Where is he now?" Remo said.

"He's on an island off the coast of New Jersey were he's hoping to stay until he dies a natural death. Privately, his doctors say that shouldn't be too long. But that isn't all. There are left-wing groups in America who want to kill him. The Russians want to prove to the world that the United States can't protect its own friends. The total price on his head might be twenty million dollars."

"What has this got to do with our skull-crusher?" Remo said.

"Well, suppose this. Suppose the man who killed Romeo was a contract killer, hired by those thugs in Brooklyn. And suppose he killed them afterwards to guard his identity."

"Yeah? So what?"

"Well, if he is a contract killer, how long do you think it's going to be before he takes a contract on the Emir?"

"I know what this is leading up to," Remo said.

"Yes, you do."

"We have to keep the Emir alive until he dies," Remo said.

"Exactly," Smith said.

"That makes marvelous sense," Remo said disgustedly. "You know . . . twenty million dollars could hire a Kamikaze squad, who'd sacrifice themselves to get the Emir. An attack like that couldn't miss."

"Maybe," said Smith.

"You want Chiun and me to protect him?"

"Not exactly," Smith said. "First, I want you to go and check his security."

"I hope it's better than the security on Romeo, or the Emir's probably already dead."

Smith winced. "Don't even joke about that. The President wants the Emir of Bislami kept alive at all costs."

"Until he dies," Remo said.

"That's correct," said Smith.

"Remo," said Chiun. "I don't understand why you have such trouble following even simple things. The Emperor is being perfectly clear."

"Thank you, Chiun," said Smith. He turned back to Remo. "Go check the Emir's security. See if you can find any holes. And then I want you to get this skull-crusher killer. We can't wait for him to come to take his shot at the Emir. Find him first."

"It shall be as you wish, Emperor," said Chiun.

Remo nodded. "But if he's dead when we get there, it's not our fault."

"Just go," said Smith, wincing again.

CHAPTER FIVE

They sat in the open cockpit of a Coast Guard launch carrying them from Sandy Hook to the Emir's island hideaway. Remo said, "You're very quiet, Chiun."

"I see," Chiun said. "When I am speaking, you interrupt me. Then, when I am quiet, you wish me to speak. So you may interrupt me again?"

"Don't bicker," Remo said. "Something's nibbling at you. What is it?"

"You are correct. Something is bothering me. It is an unpaid debt, owed to my village by the ancestors of this Emir of Bislami. His ancestors were among the most frugal . . ."

"They were cheap? With all their wealth?"

"Interrupting me is getting to be a way of life with you," Chiun said.

"I'm sorry, Little Father. Please continue."

"Thank you. It is a simple story. One I tried to tell back in Emperor Smith's office. But no one would listen."

"I'm listening already," Remo said.

"This happened many years ago, by your reckoning, when the Greekling ruled much of the East."

"The Greekling?"

"Yes. Alexander, I believe his name was. Anyway, Master Ding of Sinanju was commissioned by the Bislamic throne to remove its most dangerous of enemies. Master Ding did so, but when he returned to collect his payment, he found that the Emir, who had retained him, had died peaceably in his sleep. His son, the new Emir, refused to pay, saying the debt died with his father. It has been owed ever since. Why do you look so surprised?"

"It was really a simple story," Remo said.

"Did I not say it was?"

"Yes, but you always say that, then you go on forever and you end with some proverb that is totally confusing," Remo said.

"I never confuse. You are always confused."

"What?"

"Exactly," Chiun said. "A wonderful demonstration of my point."

"Chiun, are you going to hold the Emir responsible for his ancestor's debts?"

"I do not know. He is not the present monarch of his country. On the other hand, if he wants to return to his throne, he can hardly make much of a moral case if he goes around refusing to pay his empire's just and righteous debts. I will have to decide."

"Let me know what you decide."

Chiun nodded, then stared straight ahead at the shoreline of the small island, toward which the Coast Guard launch was racing.

They dropped ashore, off the launch, on the uninhabited side of the island. The main house faced in toward shore, and Remo had decided that the best way to test security would be to try to get to the Emir without notifying anyone they were there.

They moved up the sloping sand dune and through the scruffy clumps of ocean grass noiselessly.

41

Chiun touched Remo's shoulder and when Remo turned, the old man pointed to a sound detector wired into a bush. Remo nodded. It was clumsy but probably effective against most. Of course it would not be effective against practitioners of Sinanju, for one of the first things learned, and one of the most important lessons drilled into his head by Chiun, had been moving noiselessly.

"When one is silent," Chiun had said, "he has time to repair his mistakes. And having watched you train, you will need all the time you can get." And then he had set out a trail of peanut shells and crumpled paper and glass marbles and forced Remo to run across them, at top speed, without making a sound. And when Remo had complained after days of training that grew into months, Chiun had said simply: "No one whips the silent dog. Run."

By the time they had reached the top of the rise and could see the large house, they had run across electrified fences, mine fields, electric-eye alert systems, and rolls of barbed wire. Remo was impressed. It had not stopped him and Chiun, but nothing would have. Basically, the security was not all that bad. If the personnel had any training, Remo might even rate security as good.

Finally, he and Chiun strolled across the hundred yard open field that led to the rear of the mansion.

A guard on the door saw them and Remo and Chiun could hear him shout inside the house. Eight members of the Emir's personal guard poured from the house and raced toward them, rifles and handguns at the ready.

"Halt," one of them ordered.

"Why does everybody say 'Halt'?" Remo asked Chiun. "Why not just say 'Stop'?"

"I always like what they say in police movies," Chiun said. " 'Hold it right there, pardner.' "

"You've got them mixed up again," Remo said. He was going to explain when he felt his ribs nudged by a rifle barrel.

He turned and addressed the man with the most braid on his comic-opera uniform.

"We are from the United States government, sent to assist in the security for the Emir."

"We were not informed that your government was sending anyone," the braided man said. He wore a flat-topped, pilot-type hat, and strings of greasy hair hung out from below the brim.

"We asked that you not be notified. We wanted to test your defenses for ourselves. As you can see, we are here."

Slowly, imperceptibly, the eight guards had surrounded Remo and Chiun.

"Where is a U.S. representative?" Remo said. "He can check our credentials."

"We are perfectly capable of checking your credentials ourselves," the leader said. "We do not appreciate this intrusion."

Remo raised his hands in a gesture of wanting to reason with the spokesman. "Now listen," he started. One of the guards mistook the raised hands as an act of aggression and swung at Remo with the stock of his rifle. No one but Chiun saw Remo move, but suddenly the man was sailing over the heads of the other guards. He landed, breathless but unhurt, in a clump of bushes.

"I don't want to hurt anybody," Remo said.

"You will not hurt us," the leader said, although with more confidence than he felt. He looked behind him at his soldier, a hand-picked, trained soldier, slowly lifting himself from the bushes. He had not even seen the man move to touch the soldier. Yet he must have moved. Still, how had he managed to throw the man so far?

For a split second, there was a stalemate and then a woman stepped out onto the rear porch of the house.

She had long red hair and equally red lips. Her figure was full, but youthful, shown off neatly by a peasant blouse and a pair of designer jeans, which differed from non-designer jeans only by a label sewn onto the right rear waistband.

Remo heard someone whisper, "Princess Sarra."

The Emir's younger sister.

A Princess in jeans, Remo thought. It struck him as funny. The Emir had been overthrown by a lot of sloganeering, marching students, many of them women who had been allowed into college for the first time by the Emir's modernism. They too wore Western garb and listened to rock-'n'-roll. And they had agitated for the Emir's overthrow, calling his regime "oppressive." They had finally gotten their wish. The Emir had left the country. It had been taken over by a band of religious zealots who immediately prohibited women from wearing Western clothing. Women were also prohibited from attending college. When the ones who had protested the Emir's "oppression" had tried to march to protest these new rulings, they were beaten and raped in the streets.

As the Princess Sarra approached them, Remo saw that she was no child, but a mature woman, probably nearing forty. But she walked erect, regally and proudly, and Remo felt a stirring inside himself that for a moment he could not identify as either respect or lust.

She caught his eyes and held them. A half-smile formed on her lips.

Remo nodded. He had decided. It was lust.

"Stand aside," she told the leader of the guards.

"But, Princess . . ."

"Go inside. Bring out the American agent in charge. Go now, fool, before these two men destroy my brother's vaunted Royal Guards."

The man bowed and backed off.

"Your name?" the Princess asked Remo.

"Remo."

"Only royalty has one name. Remo what?"

"Remo Schwartzenegger," said Remo. "And this is Chiun. One name only."

"Your companion?" she asked.

Remo shook his head. "Much more," was all he said. From the corner of his eyes, he saw that Chiun was pleased with the answer.

"You claim to be representatives of your government?"

"We are."

"We will see," Princess Sarra said.

They stood, eyes locked, and Remo could feel doors opening inside of him, doors that he had thought were closed for good. Princess Sarra had green eyes. Her waist was incredibly slim. Remo wanted to look at her bosom, but he felt that some-

45

how it would seem insulting. He looked anyway and Princess Sarra smiled.

The leader of the guards reappeared from inside the house, along with a harried looking man in a tweed suit with a wide rayon tie. He was short and fat and fifty.

"What's this, what's this?" the man demanded, approaching the group.

Princess Sarra eyed the man with distinct disapproval as he stopped alongside her.

"What's going on?" he asked.

Remo took out the identification card that Smith had given him for this purpose and showed it to the man. The man inspected it carefully, looking at both sides of the card which bore the names of Remo Schwartzenegger and Chiun.

"Well?" the Princess asked.

"It seems to be in order," the man admitted.

"Seems to be? Don't you know?"

"Well, I . . . it looks okay. I don't . . ."

"We will take these men inside while you check further with your government," she said. She turned to Chiun. "Will you step inside?"

"Thank you," Chiun said. "I am old and frail and my people are so poor because of unpaid debts that . . ."

"Don't start, Chiun," cautioned Remo. "We'd be delighted to come inside," he told the Princess.

Again, the half-smile formed on her full lips and she turned and walked toward the house. Remo watched her buttocks undulate as he followed her. She was a tall woman in her high heel boots, standing almost as tall as Remo himself.

He did not mind at all. He liked tall women.

And short women.

The American agent tried to keep at the Princess's side, but her disdain for him and his company was obvious. Inside, she led them to a sitting room while the agent went off to check out Remo and Chiun's story.

"You can't go," she told the Royal Guard who had started to crowd into the room after them.

They hesitated. Their leader began to speak.

"Out," Princess Sarra ordered in a tone that allowed no discussion, and the men dutifully filed out.

"Be seated," the Princess told Remo and Chiun in a voice that was an invitation, even though the words themselves were a command.

Remo took a cushion from the couch and dropped it on the floor for Chiun. While Chiun settled himself cross-legged on the cushion, Remo relaxed back onto the couch. He felt Chiun's eyes on him, even as he looked at Princess Sarra. He knew he was in for another lecture, Number 912 in Chiun's Catalog: "How women dilute the ability of a Master of Sinanju to perform at any level of consistency." To which Remo usually delivered Pupil's Comeback Number Two: "Who cares?"

"Are you here to help my brother?" Sarra asked him.

"We are what we said," explained Remo. "We came to examine the security of this island and to see if your brother is well protected."

"Obviously, the security is severely flawed, for here you are."

"Not necessarily," Remo said.

"Either that," she said, "or you two are extraordi-

47

nary kinds of men. Are you, Remo Schwartzenegger?"

Chiun answered for him. "He isn't," Chiun said. "I am. Actually, he is kind of ordinary."

Another man entered the room. He was tall and his hair was pitch-black except for a sprinkle of gray at the temples. His eyes sparkled with intensity, and his mouth looked like a thin slit cut in paper. His skin was milk-white. He wore a small beard.

"Excuse me, Princess," he said.

"Oh, Pakir. Come in." She took the man's arm and guided him to the center of the room.

"We are not quite sure yet, Pakir, whether these gentlemen are our guests or our prisoners. Although I have some doubt about our being able to keep them prisoner if we wanted to."

"So I've heard. Fortunately we won't have to. We have checked with Washington and their authorization to be here comes directly from the White House."

"Well, then," she said and the half-formed smile that had been on her face for the past fifteen minutes blossomed wide for Remo. "In that case, let me introduce our guests. Gentlemen, this is my brother's . . . how do you say it . . . right-hand man, Perce Pakir."

"Remo Schwartzenegger," said Remo. He indicated his silent companion. "This is Chiun."

"A Chinese."

"Korean," Remo said quickly—quick enough to save Pakir's life. "Please, don't make that mistake again. He's very sensitive."

"I apologize for my effrontery," Pakir said to Chiun, bowing slightly at the waist. Chiun glared,

48

but inclined his head, acknowledging the apology.

"It is apparent from your presence that our security measures—and your country's—are rather porous."

"We were just discussing that," Sarra said.

"I must tell you that I do not appreciate the way you have been treating my men," Pakir told the Princess.

"In the first place," Sarra told him coldly, "the Royal Guards are my brother's men, not yours. Second, I speak to whom I want, how I want. If you have criticisms, voice them to my brother, later. I will not quarrel with you in front of our guests."

"As you wish, Princess," Pakir replied politely. He nodded at Remo. "The Emir would like to see both of you."

Remo and Chiun stood. Sarra told Remo, "I will join you after I've changed. My brother does not appreciate the dress of Western women." She ran her hands along the outsides of her thighs. "I, on the other hand, find it very comfortable."

"See you later, Princess," Remo told her.

She tossed her hair behind her shoulders and smiled broadly at him. "Yes. Later," she said.

Remo and Pakir watched her walk from the room. Chiun watched Remo watching and shook his head sadly. Remo smiled at the old man and shrugged. Chiun's expression remained impassive. But he slowly rose and followed Remo and Pakir from the room.

CHAPTER SIX

Even ill, even propped up in bed on pillows, the Emir was royalty. He exuded nobility. Remo noticed it even as he walked into the room.

Chiun was the only other man he had ever noticed to have that quality.

"Your Highness," Pakir said. "This is Mister Remo Schwartzenegger of the United States Government."

Again, the man had ignored Chiun.

"Your Highness, this is Chiun," Remo said. "He is my companion and very much more."

"Yes," the Emir said. "I can see that. Thank you, Pakir. You may go."

"Your Highness, I wish to point out . . ."

The emaciated figure in the bed waved a bony, weak hand at his aide-de-camp. "I am sure, Perce, that I shall be quite safe with these two gentlemen. Please leave us."

"As you wish," Pakir said. "I shall be alert, should you need me." He bowed his way from the room.

Chiun was staring intently at the man in the bed, and Remo hoped that the old Korean had not decided to hold the deposed monarch accountable for that ancient debt.

"Please," the Emir beckoned. "Come closer, both of you. My voice no longer carries as it once did."

50

Remo and Chiun moved forward to opposite sides of the bed, Chiun still staring intently at the Emir who seemed not to notice the scrutiny he was under.

"It disturbs me that you were able to breach our defenses so easily," the Emir said.

He was gray-haired and incredibly thin. The skin on his face was loose, as if his skin had been a balloon which had suddenly deflated. Remo could see that he was a very tall man, and at one time he must have been imposing, but now he was just bones and loose flesh.

"It should not disturb Your Highness," Remo told him. "No one else could have gotten through that security so easily. With a few suggestions from us, your security should be tight enough to protect you from everything short of an all-out army attack."

The man in the bed laughed dryly, not by choice but as a by-product of his illness. "I don't think anyone wants me quite that badly, yet."

"I hope not," Remo said and meant it.

"Oh, no doubt there are many who would like to see me dead, but most of them would only attempt my death if it were easy. As you know, the prospect of any effort at all being needed for a particular task will always make that task that much harder and undesirable."

"I guess that's true enough," Remo said.

"Except in the case of the fanatic," Chiun pointed out. Remo and the Emir looked at him as he spoke. "Very often, it is the difficulty of the challenge that will make the mission that much more desirable for the fanatic."

"Excellent point," the Emir said. "I salute an obviously superior knowledge."

Suddenly the man in bed was struck by some sort of pain. His face twisted in anguish and then a coughing fit shook his body with spasms. Chiun, speaking soft, comforting words in Korean, reached out and touched the ruler's chest, pressing it along the ribs.

The coughing stopped and the look on the Emir's face showed that the pain had gone, too. The contorted grimace of hurt had given way to surprise, then delight.

"What . . . what did you do?" he asked Chiun.

"A simple manipulation of muscles," Chiun said.

"Are you then a physician?"

"Not in the strict sense of the word," Remo answered for Chiun.

"But obviously you have some knowledge of medicine?" the Emir asked Chiun.

Chiun nodded.

The Emir moved around in bed, seeking a more comfortable position. Remo felt he was also trying to come to some sort of decision. When he lay still, he seemed to have made his decision.

"Will you examine me?" he asked Chiun.

Chiun looked at Remo who shrugged.

"I do not know if I would be able to tell you anything different from what your own physicians have already told you," Chiun warned the Emir.

"And none of my physicians has been able to do for me what you just did with a touch. Please. I would be forever in your debt if you would examine me. No matter what the result." The sick man's eyes met Chiun's, held them a moment, and then once again, he said "Please."

At that moment, Princess Sarra entered the room, clad in a flowing silken robe, with a thick string of diamonds around her neck.

The Emir's face lit up as he saw her. "Sarra," he called.

"Yes, my brother."

"Be a good girl. Take Mister Remo for a walk while his companion and I have a private discussion."

It sounded to Remo like a polite request, but he was learning that a royal request, no matter how politely phrased, was a command to be obeyed.

Sarra bowed slightly. "As you wish, my brother. Please join me, Remo."

"Lead on, Princess. I'll see you downstairs, Chiun." But the old Korean seemed not to have heard him. He already had his hands on the Emir's chest, pressing gently.

Walking side by side, Remo noticed that Sarra had removed her high-heeled boots because she was now noticeably shorter than he was.

"What is that about?" she asked him.

"What?"

"Your companion and my brother."

"To be perfectly honest, Princess, I don't exactly know," Remo confessed.

Sarra led him downstairs, through the house and out onto a massive, front patio of stone, surrounded by an equally massive, overgrown garden. In the center of the garden was a large fountain. They sat on a stone bench looking at the water.

"Do you live out here all the time?" Remo asked.

"No, I have an apartment in New York City. Actually, I am here very little of the time. I get bored very easily."

"Pakir seems as if he'd be able to get along with your not being here. He seems to resent you."

"Pakir is in love with me," she said, "but he has a great deal of pride. A woman should be a woman and not put her nose in men's affairs. Actually, I am not the least bit interested in his affairs." She turned to look at Remo and said, "I have my own affairs to think of."

She touched Remo's hand and then smiled.

"What's funny?" he said.

"I would have expected sparks to leap from my hands to yours," she said.

"So would I," said Remo. He moved closer to her and touched a spot on her back with his fingertips, rotating them slightly. She arched her back like a stroked kitten.

"I'd like you to come visit me," she said, closing her eyes to the slight pressure of Remo's fingertips. "At my apartment. Some time soon."

"Very soon," Remo promised.

When she opened her eyes again to look at him, she looked abruptly past him, then straightened up stiffly. Remo followed her eyes and saw Chiun watching them impassively from the terrace.

"You and he," she observed. "You belong together, somehow."

"Yes," Remo said. "We are joined by thousands of years of tradition."

"But leave him behind when you visit me in New York," she said.

"Your wish is my command, sugar," he said as he got up and walked to Chiun.

"What's the story, Chiun? Will he make it?"

Chiun shook his head. "He will die, and much sooner than everyone thinks."

"You told him that?"

"Do you think I am insensitive? I told him that I could find nothing different from the findings of his own physicians. He accepted that." Chiun stared stolidly out at the sea.

"You've been acting strange since we got here," Remo said, "and even funnier since we met the Emir. Did you finally decide to hold him responsible for that debt?"

Chiun glared at him angrily. "Since you seem so concerned, I will tell you what is bothering me." He pointed toward the ceiling with a bony, long-nailed finger. "That man is a great man, a great monarch. A Master of Sinanju knows a true monarch when he meets one. That man was born to rule and what has been happening to him these past few months is beneath contempt. It is better that he die than live in exile."

"That's what happens to people who trust the United States. The quickest way to the boneyard is to figure on us to help you out." Remo paused. "Chiun . . . you didn't . . ."

"I took no action to put him out of this misery caused by your government," Chiun said coldly. "I have told you, he will die soon enough."

Remo let his air out in a sigh of relief.

"All right, then. Let's get Pakir and tell him how to beef up his security and maybe we can give the Emir the opportunity to do just that."

55

CHAPTER SEVEN

Remo's advice to Perce Pakir was simple.

"Get dogs," he said. "You've just got too much island to cover. If you put dogs on both flanks of the island, it'll force an invader to come in through the middle. That way, your devices have a better chance of picking him up."

Pakir listened politely but without enthusiasm. His coolness didn't bother Remo. When they got back, he would pass his recommendation on to Smith and, whether he liked it or not, Perce Pakir would have dogs.

The Coast Guard launch returned to pick them up at the main dock at the shore side of the island to take them to the Brooklyn dock where the two hoodlums' bodies had been found.

Remo used the ship-to-shore telephone to reach Smith at his headquarters in Folcroft Sanitarium.

"How does it look?" Smith asked.

"Not bad," Remo said. "The chief of security there doesn't like us, but I told him to get dogs."

"That's Pakir," Smith said.

"Right."

"I'll see they get dogs," Smith said.

"And who's the hoople there representing us?" Remo asked.

"That's Agent Randisi."

"FBI?" asked Remo.

"Yes."

"Check him out. He couldn't find his foot inside his shoe. He wasn't even around when we were discussing the security with Pakir."

"How is the big man?" Smith said.

Remo knew who he meant. "Impressive, but not long for this world. He'll die in bed."

"If he has to die, that's the way I'd prefer it," Smith said.

"Did you find out anything about the men on the dock?"

"They were shopping for an assassin to take out Romeo," Smith said. "It appears they found one."

"Any idea who?" Remo asked Smith.

"No," said Smith. "It might even have been an amateur. All the professionals seemed to have been frightened off. See what you can find."

"Okay, Smitty."

They were almost at their destination when Remo broke off the connection, and a few minutes later they were prowling the smelly, dirty pier.

"This looks like the spot, Chiun," said Remo.

"Look with more than your eyes, meat-eater," Chiun said. There were dark stains in the wood of the dock, apparently blood stains. Remo crouched down to look at them.

"I don't even know what we're looking for," Remo complained.

Chiun squatted next to him, looking over the area. He reached out with his hand and ran it over the stains.

"Something is stuck in the wood," he said.

Remo watched as Chiun's skillful fingers dug at the wood of the dock and lifted it free.

57

"There," said Chiun, holding his hand open to Remo.

"There what?" said Remo. All he could see was a black speck, a chip of something in Chiun's hand.

"Have you ever seen anything that black?" Chiun asked.

"Only the inside of a Chinaman's heart," Remo said.

"A worthy sentiment, but mistimed. Pay attention. Look at that chip of paint carefully."

"So it's very black," Remo said. He looked again. "Very, very black. And again, so what?"

"I have never seen anything so black," Chiun said. "This reflects no light at all."

"I really don't get what this is all about."

"Something that black would be invisible in the dark," Chiun said. "It would reflect nothing back to the eye. Does that answer your question?"

"You mean to tell me that we're dealing with a guy who has an invisible kind of paint? Somebody's painting himself invisible?"

"It is possible," Chiun said.

"Jesus," said Remo. "Smitty's going to love this one."

He had spent his life afraid of the dark, but now Elmo Wimpler knew that the light was his enemy. In the dark, in blackness, he was God, a King, ruler of all he surveyed. But in the light, he would be just another small man in a dark cloth suit. He would be a wimp again.

Never. Never again.

He had tasted power, killing those three men—an

58

incredible feeling of power beyond anything he had ever felt before.

He would not give up that power. The power to do anything. To buy anything. To have any woman. To decide life and death for others.

His only enemy was the light.

In the garage attached to his small home, Wimpler inspected his black, invisibility outfit and found a small piece of paint had chipped off. He would have to work on that. Perhaps he could make the paint with a rubber or latex base so it would be flexible and would not crack or chip. He sprayed the flaked spot again.

The outfit was as good as new.

He wanted to use it again.

He couldn't wait to use it again.

And he knew just who to use it on.

He had a couple of debts to pay back.

While the outfit was drying, he looked on his shelves for an invention he had been working on several years before. It was an electronic oscillator. Aimed at a power source, it would jam the electrical current, changing its frequency, and the surge of power would blow out lights all along the line of the circuit. It had worked but it had no commercial value. Who would want to blow out lights?

So Wimpler had put it on a shelf and forgotten it. Until now. He found the small box and inserted a fresh, nine-volt battery. Then he aimed it at a small, night light he kept burning in the garage. There was no sound, but suddenly the light went off.

Elmo Wimpler laughed aloud. He sprayed the unit with his black invisibility paint, and then began to put on his special suit.

59

It was time to visit his neighbors, Curt and Phyllis. He planned to spend a little more time with Phyllis than with Curt, though. He figured to be done with Curt very quickly. Very quickly.

Getting into the house was easy. The storm door to the rear hallway was unlocked. He walked in and stood in the dark hallway, watching Phyllis doing the dinner dishes. He enjoyed the view. She was wearing a backless halter top and he admired the arch of her spine as it sloped down to her behind which was clad only in a pair of pink panties. Her long legs were covered by a thin sheen of perspiration on the hot night. Her feet were bare, her ankles trim and lovely, and she was humming a tune as she worked. Even with the teased hair and loud mouth, she was quite a woman. She had always been Elmo's one main sexual fantasy. He had imagined himself doing unimaginable things to her and tonight, after he was done with Curt, he would do all of them.

To his left were the basement steps and Elmo could hear Curt down there grunting, doing his usual nightly weight-lifts. He took a last lingering look at Phyllis's back and then went quietly down the steps to the basement.

Curt was on his back doing bench presses with a 150-pound barbell. As Wimpler watched, Curt pushed the bar up overhead, locked his elbows, then let the bar down to rest on his chest. When the barbell was over his head, Elmo aimed his power oscillator at the single overhead light. Instantly, the cellar plunged into darkness.

"Shit," Curt growled. "Freaking light blew."

Wimpler was already standing behind him, his skull-crusher out and open.

60

"Curt," he said softly.

"What? Who's there?" The fear in his voice gave Wimpler almost an electric thrill down his spine.

"Just visiting like a good neighbor," Wimpler said. He had the skull-crusher around Curt's head. "Good-bye, neighbor," he said, as he pressed the button. He heard the phhhhht of the compressor and then the cracking sound of Curt's skull.

Curt did not even have time to yell.

Wimpler stood at the bottom of the steps.

He held his hand over his mouth and called loudly, "Phyllis," trying to imitate Curt's loud roar.

From the shadows he could see the woman standing at the top of the cellar stairs.

"Curt? Why's it dark down there?"

Again muffling his voice, Wimpler yelled, "Come on down."

Gamely, she came down the steps to the cellar. Wimpler let her pass him, then ran noiselessly up the steps to close the top cellar door, to keep out all light.

Then he was back downstairs, invisible in the blackness, standing behind her.

"Curt?" she called softly. This time there was a little question in her voice.

Elmo put his arms around her. She thought it was Curt. She purred.

Wimpler hit her alongside the head, just before putting the gag in her mouth, just before he went to work to make all his fantasies come true.

CHAPTER EIGHT

"Another one?" Remo asked.

"Just like the others. Skull crushed," Smith said. He gave Remo the Brooklyn address.

"Anything on that paint chip?" Remo asked.

"Not yet. It's still in the laboratory. I'll let you know what we find out."

Remo hung up and looked out the window at Manhattan. He had moved into this midtown hotel to be close to Princess Sarra, and now he was off again to Brooklyn.

And he didn't like Brooklyn. He had never liked Brooklyn. When he was a boy in the orphanage, the nuns had made them read a short story titled "Only the Dead Know Brooklyn."

In a test, they had asked for the name of the story, and he had written, "Only the Dumb Like Brooklyn." For that smart-ass answer, he had gotten himself rapped on the knuckles with a ruler. He had resented Brooklyn ever since.

When they arrived at the address, they saw a small, mild-looking man walking out of the house next door. He was carrying a cardboard carton to a rented Haul-It-Ur-Self which was parked in front of his house.

As the little man neared the van, he tripped and started to fall. Remo reached out for the carton and helped the man maintain his balance. When Remo helped him get the heavy carton into the van, the little man turned to him and thanked him effusively.

"Don't mention it," Remo said. "Moving out?"

"Yes, sir. The crime rate is becoming much too high in this area to go on living here. Especially after what happened next door."

"Do you know those people well?" Remo asked.

Elmo Wimpler shook his head. "Not really. Just to say hello in the morning. You know, neighbor stuff." He shook his head, as if still disbelieving the facts. "What a terrible thing to happen. A murder right next door to my house."

"Murder?" Remo asked. "I thought the police still called it a questionable death."

"I don't know what they call it, but I know that Phyllis—that's Curt's wife—has been telling the whole neighborhood that he was murdered and she was . . . uh, sexually abused."

The little man looked embarrassed even to say the words. Remo pitied him instantly. What kind of boring life must this little man live?

"Did you hear any noises last night? Remo asked.

"I didn't hear a thing, but I'm in bed early and I'm a very sound sleeper. Phyllis says she screamed, but I didn't hear it. I'm really sorry about that."

"Maybe you're lucky," Remo said, patting the man on the shoulder. "You might have been the next victim."

The man visibly shuddered. "I want to finish my packing," he said quickly.

"Go ahead. Thanks."

The little man went back toward the house and Remo joined Chiun.

"That little man does not like his neighbors," the old Korean said.

"Who does? Let's visit Phyllis."

Mourning for her dead husband had not made Phyllis any more sedate in her choice of clothing. She was wearing short shorts and a T-shirt top when she answered the door. The body wasn't bad, Remo thought, and if only she had taken care of her face, she might even have been passable-looking.

"Whaddya want?" she demanded.

"We're here about your husband," Remo said.

In spite of her recent loss, Phyllis looked twice at Remo and liked what she saw. He wasn't big, like Curt, but there was something masculine about him, something that made her tingle.

"You a cop?" she asked.

Remo smiled. "We're concerned with who killed your husband."

Like most people, she had asked a question and not listened to the answer. She assumed that Remo had said he was a cop. She looked at Chiun. "He a cop, too?" she asked Remo.

"Not exactly," Remo said. "Much more than that." He was rewarded by a faint smile from Chiun. "May we come in?"

She thought about it for a moment, then said, "I guess so," and backed up. When Remo passed her, he deliberately brushed against her. Chiun followed and she closed the door behind them.

"Can I get you something?" she asked. "Coffee? A drink?"

"No thanks. We don't want to take up too much of your time. Could you show us where it happened?"

"I . . . I don't want to go down there. I'll show you where it is. You can go down."

As she led them to the cellar steps, Remo noticed that the back storm door was unlocked.

"That always unlocked?" he asked.

She stared at him wide-eyed, then reached past him and flipped on the lock.

"A bad habit," she said. "One I guess I'll have to break."

Barn doors, thought Remo. She stayed in the kitchen as they went downstairs.

The police had made a half-hearted attempt to clean the blood and brains off the floor. There was a rumpled blanket in a corner and it was obvious from the stains on it what it had been used for.

Remo effortlessly moved the barbells aside and examined the stains on the floor. Chiun was hunched over the blanket in the corner.

After a thorough investigation, lasting at least four seconds, Remo stood up and said, "I don't see anything."

Without turning, Chiun said, "Come here, white thing."

Remo went over and crouched next to him.

"Find something?"

"Look." Chiun held out his hand. It was another paint chip.

"Ties it all together," Remo said. "Same killer. And we still don't know anything about him."

"We will learn," Chiun said. "Or at any rate, I will learn and I will tell you all about it."

Remo put the paint chip in his shirt pocket and followed Chiun upstairs. Phyllis had fixed her face and hair while they were in the cellar. She didn't look half bad now, Remo thought. Unless she was compared with Princess Sarra, in which case she was a distant also-ran.

"Did you hear anything before you heard your husband call you?"

"No. Nothing."

"Were the lights on in the cellar?" Chiun asked.

"No. The light was out."

"Thank you," Remo said. "You've been very helpful."

"If you need anything else, you just call," she told Remo, smiling and touching her teased hair. Then she seemed to remember she was a very recent widow and she touched her nose with her handkerchief. She walked them to the door and whispered to Remo, "Is he really a cop? You can tell me."

"Actually," Remo said, "He's a CIA agent, but that's very confidential."

"Wow," Phyllis said. As they opened the door to the steps, they saw the little man next door, finishing loading his van.

"Him," she snapped.

"What about him?" Remo asked.

"If these criminals didn't think that all the houses were owned by pissy-faced little wimps like him, this kind of thing wouldn't happen. Curt would still be alive."

Was she actually trying to blame that helpless, innocent little guy next door for her husband's death, Remo wondered.

"I'm sure you're right," he said. "Thank you for your time."

"Least I could do," she said. "Call me if you need me." She put an extra emphasis on the word "need."

"Sure will," Remo said. As he and Chiun started down the walk, she stepped out and began yelling.

"Little nothing. Why couldn't it have been you instead of Curt, you little nothing?"

Remo looked over at the little man who was just standing there, staring at the screaming woman.

Poor little guy.

After Remo and Chiun had driven off, Elmo Wimpler reached into his jacket pocket and took out a small, pink, flimsy piece.

He shook it out and held it up in plain sight. It was a pair of pink, woman's panties.

After displaying it for a few seconds, he kissed it and threw it into one of the cartons in the back of the van.

Phyllis had caught the whole scene. She held her breath. Her panties had been ripped off her the night before by the phantom rapist-murderer.

But no, it couldn't be. Not Wimpler.

She watched as he locked up his house and went back to the van. Before getting in, he turned her way and threw her a wave and a kiss.

No, she thought, hugging her arms. It couldn't be. It just couldn't be.

CHAPTER NINE

There were a lot of contracts to fill and a lot of millions to make in his new profession, but first Elmo Wimpler had one more personal piece of business to take care of.

Actually, three pieces of business.

The three owners of the Friends of Inventors were in their office late, studying the books on the week's take, when suddenly the lights in the room went out.

The door to the room opened and closed quickly.

Ernie, sitting in the middle of the table, heard a grunt from the partner on his right and felt something wet strike him on the shoulder. He turned to look at his partner and in the dimness of the office, he saw his partner had only half a head. And the wet stuff, suddenly he knew, was blood.

He turned to his left, in time to hear a phhhhht sound and the snap of bone and his partner's grunt as his half-head slumped forward and hit the large, oaken table.

"What the fuck," he said, jumping up from his seat and looking around him. He saw nothing.

"Sorry I couldn't come up with anything in mauve," a voice said to him from out of the emptiness.

"Who's that?" Ernie stuttered.

He felt himself pushed from behind. He turned quickly but no one was there.

"I'm going apeshit nuts," he said aloud.

"Ever sell that car of yours?" the disembodied voice asked.

Something slapped Ernie in the face, but again there was no one to see.

"I'm dreaming," he said.

"No, you're not," the voice said.

"What is this?" Ernie demanded in a voice made loud with fear.

"Just think mauve," the voice said. Ernie felt some kind of touch on his head and just before he died, he remembered the meeting they had had with the wimpy looking guy with the funny black paint. No. It couldn't be him. Could it?"

Phhhhhhht. Crack.

"Three more?" Remo asked Smith from the phone in his New York hotel room, overlooking Central Park.

"That's right," said Smith and gave Remo the address of the Friends of Inventors. "It's a phony operation that takes money from would-be inventors but it doesn't market anything."

"All crushed skulls?" Remo asked.

"Correct," Smith said. "But there was something else too. There was a note written in mauve-colored paint on the table."

"What'd the note say?" Remo asked.

"It said, 'This is the last one I do for free.'"

"And another amateur succumbs to the lure of money and turns pro," Remo said.

"And for a pro, the only game in town is the Emir of Bislami," Smith said. "Chiun was right about the paint by the way. It's a special metallic compound that absorbs all light hitting it."

"Would it make someone invisible?"

"In the dark," Smith said. "All you could see is a black outline against a lighter background. But you couldn't pick up any details because they wouldn't send any light to your eye."

"But in daylight?"

"In daylight, if our man were wearing some kind of painted costume like this," Smith said, "you would see the black silhouette of a man. Almost like a shadow."

"Then he can't function in the light," Remo said.

"No. I don't see how he could," Smith agreed.

"Remember I told you to get dogs for the Emir's island?" Remo said.

"Yes. They're already there."

"Install floodlights, too," Remo said. "All over. Make the place look like Yankee Stadium during a night game."

"That's a good idea," Smith said.

The words were so strange to Remo's ear that he said, "Say that again."

"I said that was a good idea," Smith said.

"Now I can die happy," Remo said.

"Don't die at all. And don't let anyone else die," Smith said as he hung up the telephone.

Remo replaced the receiver and turned to Chiun.

"Three more."

"So I heard. I am not yet so old that my ears fail to function. The Emperor seemed worried."

"He is worried about the Emir," Remo said.

70

"We have never opposed an invisible man before," Chiun said.

Remo scowled. "Just a guy in a black suit."

"You can wish that," Chiun said. "But there are six people with only pieces left of their skulls who would not agree with you."

For all the mayhem that had been committed in the conference room of the Friends of Inventors, the room looked as if it had been sent out to the dry cleaners for washing and pressing.

The rug was spotless. Chairs were neatly placed around the table. Blackboards for chart presentations were neatly stacked against a wall.

The only note that seemed out of place in this symphony of order was the note written in paint on the conference table. "This is the last one I do for free."

Mauve, Smith had called it.

"Chiun," Remo said. The Korean did not answer. Remo looked up and saw Chiun standing at the light switch. He flicked it and the overhead chandelier lights went off. He flicked the switch again. The lights came back on.

Again. Off.

Again. On.

"Chiun, when you're finished inventing electricity, will you come here?" Remo said.

The Korean walked smoothly toward the table.

"See this. The purple paint. That's the note the killer left," Remo said.

Chiun shook his head. "No," he said.

"What do you mean 'no'?"

"That's not purple. It's mauve," Chiun said.

Remo decided it was mauve. But it still looked like purple.

"Why were you fooling around with the light?" Remo asked.

"I was trying to learn something," Chiun said.

"What was it?"

"I have not yet learned it," Chiun said.

Remo stepped into the outer office where the blonde receptionist sat preening herself. Stacked in front of her was a comb, fingernail polish, liquid makeup, mascara, and four different kinds of lipstick and lip gloss.

"Ain't it a tragedy?" she said to Remo.

"I can see you're having trouble bearing up."

"They wasn't bad. I mean, for those kind," she said. She breathed her chest at Remo, who wondered if good manners would dictate his fleeing in fright to the other side of the room.

"Who was here last night when this happened?" Remo asked.

"Just Willy, the janitor. He was cleaning one of the other offices. Want me to get him?"

"Please. And then I want you to go through your files," Remo said. "Get me the name and address of everybody who's been here in the past six months. Every client. And what they invented."

"Geez. That could take a half-hour maybe."

"Do it and I'll put you in for overtime," Remo said. "But call Willy first."

Willy the janitor had white hair, bifocals and a scowl that looked genetic.

"Did you hear anything last night, Willy?" Remo asked. "Or see anything?"

"Well," the old man said. He clamped his lips shut as if that constituted a full answer.

"Willy, it's important that you tell us," Remo said.

"What's in it for me?" Willy said.

"Let me discuss this with Mister Willy," Chiun whispered. "You don't know how to talk to old people." His green satin kimono flowed around him as he walked to the old man.

His hand darted out of his sleeve and he caught Willy's right ear between two fingers.

"Now answer questions," Chiun said.

"Owwwww. Yes sir."

"Willy will help now," Chiun said.

"I'm really glad you understand the mature mind," Remo said.

"All minds are alike where pain is concerned," Chiun said.

Once started talking, there seemed to be no way to quiet Willy the janitor.

"I didn't want anyone to think I was senile, but I heard it. I heard a voice. And it wasn't one of the voices of the partners 'cause I knew them voices 'cause they all sound like Long Island, but this voice wasn't like that, but when I went inside I didn't see nothing, but I know I heard it. And I ain't senile either. And I heard him say, 'This is the last one I do for free.' But I didn't see anybody. And then I had to call the police, and then I cleaned up that mess. It was awful, somebody left me this bloody, stinking mess and you don't know how long it took me to get that room clean again."

"But you saw nobody."

"Just them bodies. Awful it was, brains and all, all over."

"The voice you heard. What did it sound like?"

"Just a voice. Soft like. But a man's voice. A soft, man's voice, like he was a whisperer, like you know how some people are."

Willy was still rubbing his ear. "Can I go now?"

"I'm done with you," Remo said.

"I am not," Chiun said. Willy clapped his hands over his ears in self-defense.

"Unhand your ears, you idiot," Chiun said. "When you came into this office last night, were the lights on or off?"

Remo shook his head. Chiun's lights again.

"The switch was on," said Willy. "But all the lights was off. Nine of them. Count them. Nine of those bulbs. They was all burned out. And they was new bulbs, 'cause I only changed them like a month ago. I change all the bulbs at once 'cause I read a story once that it's more efficient to do it that way than to let them burn out and change them one at a time."

"So the bulbs were extinguished and you replaced them?" Chiun repeated.

"That's right, sir. Yes, sir. That's right."

"You may go," Chiun said, dismissing Willy with a wave of his long-nailed hands.

"That's handling those old folks, Chiun," said Remo after Willy left. "You call that respect?"

"Respect, unlike water, runs from low place to high place. This means that you should respect everyone you meet. I, on the other hand, am to be treated with respect by everyone. You may not like it, Remo, but it is the way of things."

"Make your next lecture on modesty," Remo growled. "You do it so well. Why are you so interested in the light bulbs?"

"Because our invisible man," Chiun said, "can only be effective in the darkness. These last killings and the one of that man with the wife who varnished her hair were done in darkness. Darkness created by the killer. He may have a way, Remo, to turn out lights."

Remo nodded. The old Korean made sense.

"Then I guess we better turn out his lights and fast," Remo said.

The secretary in the outer office had overestimated the difficulty of compiling the names, addresses, and inventions of all the clients the firm had seen in the last six months. There were only twenty of them and she finished the job in twenty-eight minutes.

Remo sat at the conference table looking at the sheet of yellow paper on which she had printed in large block letters the client list.

He did not know what, if anything, he was looking for. But without leads, he would settle for anything. A clue. A hint. A hunch. Anything.

And it was there. The third name on the list.

"Chiun. Look at this." The Korean came over and stood behind Remo's shoulder.

"Invisible paint," Remo read. "Elmo Wimpler. And look at the address. Right next door to the guy with the varnished wife."

"The little man who did not like his neighbors," Chiun said.

"You're right," Remo said. Somehow he had failed to associate the name and address with the man they had met earlier. "The little nerd with the rented van."

"The little ones are often the most dangerous," Chiun said.

Remo looked at Chiun, who stood less than five feet tall, but suppressed the smile he felt that remark deserved.

"I think we ought to go back to Wimpler's house and see what we see," Remo said.

"Or cannot see," Chiun said.

CHAPTER TEN

Elmo Wimpler had left his furniture behind when he left his ramshackle Brooklyn home. Looking around, Remo could understand why. His couch was a massive, flower-covered lump in which a normal person, if he made the mistake of sitting down, might vanish without a trace. The living room armchairs were ratty and ripped.

His kitchen set was a small, round table with one wobbly leg and a hard-backed chair with a worn-through cushion. His bedroom set was ornate, old wood that looked as if it had been carved during the First Crusade.

Remo went through the house carefully, room by room, looking for something, anything, that would tell him who Elmo Wimpler was, and, more important, where he was.

But every personal trace seemed to have disappeared. There were no boxes of letters in the basement, no high-school yearbooks, no correspondence with relatives. Nothing that would indicate that the house had been lived in any time since the Industrial Revolution.

But when he got back to the living room, Chiun had found something Remo had missed.

The old man was sitting cross-legged on the floor, reading through a magazine. Next to him on the threadbare rug was a small pile of other magazines. They had apparently been stashed under the couch.

Remo looked through the stack of magazines. Four of them were girlie magazines for the sadomasochistic trade. But the other three were copies of a magazine called *Contract*.

Remo looked at the one Chiun was looking through. The cover showed a diplomat, in striped trousers and formal coat, standing on a street corner. A man behind him was looping a strangler's wire over the diplomat's head. The cover blazed the legend of what was inside. "New Techniques for Successful Assassination." And "The Most Wanted Man in the World."

"I have never heard of this magazine," said Chiun.

"Me neither. Is it what I think it is?"

"It is for your American excuses-for-assassins. It tells them who somebody wants to have killed and what the fees are."

"Did the 'New Techniques for Successful Assassination' teach you anything?" Remo asked.

"Only that you and I never need fear being out of work," Chiun said. "Here." He handed the magazine forward. "You will find this interesting."

The magazine was opened to the article: "The Most Wanted Man in the World." Accompanying the article was a photograph of the Emir of Bislami in full military regalia.

The article said there was a twenty-million-dollar price on the deposed Emir's head, and the article's title had been circled in red ink.

Remo looked through the rest of the magazine. The classified section in the front was circled in red pen. He turned to the classified section and glanced at the help wanted columns:

WANTED: FEMALE WITH ABILITY TO KILL WITH PLEASURE. RESUME AND REFERENCES NECESSARY.

The ad gave a box number.

There were ads advertising different killing specialties: throwing knives, ripping knives, crossbows, undetectable poisons, guns with special night sights.

Another item circled in red caught Remo's eyes:

EVER KILL AN EMIR? CHECK OUT THE PRICE. (Another box number.)

Another read:

ICE AN EMIR. (A box number.)

A third read:

SEND A MONARCH TO THE MORTUARY.

"Chiun," Remo started.

"I have seen them," Chiun said. He was reading another issue of *Contract* magazine. He seemed engrossed. Remo put the copy of the magazine into his back pocket and stood up to check the garage.

He went out the back door of the house and walked to the small detached garage. He saw the widow, Phyllis, in the next yard. When she saw him, her hand went naturally to her teased, blond hair.

"You couldn't stay away, could you?" she said with a smile.

"Just checking a few more things," he told her.

"Come in for coffee or something when you're through. Maybe I can help you with a few things."

"Sorry. I'm on duty right now," Remo said.

"When you get off duty," she said.

"Maybe. We'll see."

She chose to take his answer as agreement, smiled, and turned back to her gardening.

Remo entered the dark garage, made black even in the daytime by the heavy plastic sheets that covered the windows.

He found an overhead light and flipped it on.

Against the far wall, he saw a large workbench. The shelves that lined the walls were filled with gadgets and devices, apparently the lifework of a committed inventor. Each item was labeled, with the date of its creation.

There were mousetraps that looked like lobster traps. There was a disco light radio. Another item was labelled "Electric Shoe Softener." It was a big metal foot, and from its hinging, Remo guessed that when it was plugged in, the foot bent and stretched, wearing out the stiffness of any new shoe placed on the device.

Two spots were empty. The sign at one spot said "Pneumatic Nut Cracker." The other sign read: "Electric Light Oscillator."

The poured concrete floor of the garage was stained different colors. Some places showed the evidence of burning. In other spots, there were holes chipped into the floor. Probably all by-products of one invention or another, Remo thought.

The center of the garage was taken up with an old wreck of a car, dented, rusted, and obviously painted over quickly with a light-blue spray enamel.

Why would anyone have bothered to paint such a wreck of a car, Remo wondered. And why paint it so badly?

He leaned on the car and thought for a moment. The only reason to paint a car that quickly and carelessly was to disguise it. But what had it been before that it needed a disguise? There wasn't much difference between an ugly, old blue car and an ugly, old red or green or black car.

Black car.

Remo turned back to the car and began to examine it carefully. In the corners around the windshield, he could see traces of a deep black paint. There were the same marks around the headlights and taillights.

He found a reasonably smooth section of fender and chipped away at it with his fingertips. He was right. Underneath the blue paint was black, and as he chipped away at more and more, he could see that the black paint was the deep, invisibility black that Chiun had found a chip of earlier.

He left the garage and went straight back to Wimpler's house, pointedly ignoring the posturing and posing of Phyllis in her garden.

Chiun was still reading *Contract*.

"You were right, Chiun," Remo said.

"Of course. What this time?"

"He must have tested his invisible paint on the old car in his garage."

"We knew he had invented that paint."

"But he also invented a nutcracker and something to do with electric lights," Remo said.

"The skull-crusher and the device for burning out electric lamps," Chiun said.

Remo nodded.

"Now that I have done all your work for you," said Chiun, "don't you think you owe me some small favor?"

"Such as."

"Find out who the editor is of this magazine," Chiun said.

"Why?"

"Because if they pay their writers for these awful tales and essays, think how proud and happy they would be to have me writing for them."

"I don't think they're into Ung poetry," Remo said.

"I am not talking about poetry, but about a different kind of beauty. They write about assassins and removals, and who could write about these subjects better than I?"

"No one, I guess," said Remo. He had a sinking feeling in his stomach. He had thought that Chiun had given up on trying to write for a living. But that was a mistake. Chiun had just been waiting for his chance. Writers never quit.

"Good," said Chiun. "You find out about this publication. I will write for them and you will be my agent. Three percent of all I earn shall be yours."

"Oh, joy," said Remo. "I'm going to be wealthy."

CHAPTER ELEVEN

The New York Telephone Company had built its reputation on taking sixty days to install a telephone and begin service, and only sixty seconds to disconnect a phone. But in his hurried move from his Brooklyn house, Elmo Wimpler obviously had not notified the company, because the telephone in the bedroom was still turned on.

When he reached Smith, there was agitation in the CURE director's voice.

"Where have you been?" Smith said. "I've been trying to reach you."

"Easy. You'll live longer," Remo said. "Besides, we've been out here solving this case. Your killer is a little twerp named Elmo Wimpler. He invented the invisible paint. He also invented some kind of skull-crusher machine and a gadget that blows out lights. He lived next door to that Curt who got it last night, and those three guys at the Friends of Inventors had turned down his paint invention."

"Where is he now?" Smith said.

"I don't know. He split from his house in Brooklyn," Remo said. "Anyway," he continued. "That's the good news. Now the bad news."

"Go ahead. I'm used to it from you," Smith said.

"There's a magazine called *Contract*," Remo said.

"I've heard of it."

"We found some copies of it in Wimpler's house. A lot of stuff in there involved killing the Emir, and he had them circled. Stories, ads and things." Remo still had the copy of the magazine in his pocket. He took it out and read some of the ads to Smith.

"Here's one called 'Ice an Emir,'" Remo said.

"That one is mine," Smith said.

"What?"

"I placed that one," Smith said. "That's what I was calling about."

"You're responsible for 'Ice an Emir'? I didn't think you had it in you," Remo said.

"I was second in my class at Dartmouth in creative writing," Smith said.

"Well, don't think I'm going to be your agent, too," Remo said. "I've already got a client."

"I placed that advertisement to try to flush out anybody who might be thinking about a contract killing on the Emir," Smith said.

"I got my first group of answers today. Most of them are obvious cranks, but one in particular seemed real. I think it might be our friend, Wimpler. I'm supposed to meet him tonight," Smith said.

"Where?" asked Remo.

"In the Sheep Meadow at Central Park. At midnight."

"We'll take it for you, Smitty," Remo said.

"I don't have to tell you how important this is," Smith said.

"Then don't," Remo said. It was the same old thing, a sidewise slide by Smith into telling Remo that he was not to bring Wimpler back alive. Smith's rock-bound, New England morality made it difficult for him to order Remo to kill someone, but over the years he had found enough ways to say it without saying it. What Smith wanted was Elmo Wimpler's body left lying in Central Park. It wasn't a question of trying to evade responsibility. Remo had seen the pills that Smith always carried and was prepared to use, pills that would kill Smith in seconds. Remo had seen the coffin in the basement of Folcroft, in which Smith's body would go, and be sent to a funeral home in Parsippany, New Jersey, for a fast prepaid funeral. If Remo knew one thing in the world, it was that Smith would not try to run away from his responsibilities.

It was something else. It was simply the conflict between Smith's heart-deep belief in obeying the law, and his equally strong belief that CURE, while working outside the law, was absolutely necessary if America was to survive. He was unable to reconcile the two. He managed to deal with it by talking around it. Instead of directing Remo to kill Wimpler, he just reminded him how important it was. And Remo was well-trained. He knew what the assignment was. Elmo Wimpler had to die, and Smith would be happy about the result, and able to cling to some small piece of his pre-CURE self by knowing that he had not ordered the death. Not in so many words anyway.

Out in the living room, Remo told Chiun, "Come on. We're taking a walk in Central Park tonight."

Chiun rose, like a puff of smoke, still reading the copy of *Contract* he held in his hands.

He followed Remo toward the front door. Remo politely held the door open for him and Chiun stepped out first.

Then Remo heard it. It was a sound above them. Chiun's eyes were burrowed into the magazine. Remo could hear the feet on the edge of the roof above them. He heard the scraping as the feet pushed from the edge of the roof.

Someone was coming at Chiun. From off the roof. And the old man, oblivious, his nose stuck in that magazine, was an easy victim. Remo jumped out through the open front door, pivoted around and met the attacker as he came from the low roof in a flying leap. Remo caught him around the waist. The sound of the man's spine filled the dark quiet street with a loud snap.

Remo let the man drop to the sidewalk. Chiun continued walking away without looking up.

"There is another one up there, too," he said over his shoulder to Remo.

Remo glanced upward in time to see a second man, a knife in his hand, leap off the roof toward Remo. Remo ducked, grabbed the man who lay in a clump on the walk, and tossed him up.

The quick and the dead collided in midair. And then both were dead as the knife in the live man's hand twisted around from the force of the collision and buried itself in the man's throat. They were both dead when the two bodies hit again.

Remo glanced up. Chiun was leaning against their rented car, still reading.

Remo looked through the dead men's clothing. There was no identification. Their faces told him nothing. They could have been any of a half-dozen nationalities. There were no wallets, no clothing tags, no driver's licenses. Nothing.

Remo left the bodies where they lay. When he approached the car, Chiun said, "What took you so long?"

"You could have warned me they were up there," Remo groused.

"I was busy reading. Why is it that people in this country always think that if you're reading, you are not doing anything important?" He pointed over Remo's shoulder. "And my magazines. You dropped them. Go pick them up. First, you keep me waiting, and then you drop my magazines, too. Really, Remo."

Back at their hotel room, high overlooking Central Park, Remo called Smith again and told him of the attack at Wimpler's house.

"No identification at all?" Smith asked.

"None," Remo said.

"Could you tell if they were foreign?"

"You mean, maybe from the Emir Bislami? I don't know. They could have been from Italy for all I know."

"Dark skinned?" Smith asked.

"Yes, but that means Spanish, Italian, Bislamic, or a dozen other things including sun tanned. Besides, why would anyone from Bislami send a hit team after Chiun and me?"

"Maybe you didn't make any friends when you visited the Emir?" Smith said. "Be careful tonight."

"Sure, Daddy. Tell Mommy we love her. Bye."

Chiun was still reading *Contract* in the living room of the hotel apartment.

"Did you see any ads that might fit us?" Remo asked him.

"No. Not one. Not once did I see any advertisement calling for someone to attempt fruitlessly, to

87

dispatch the Master of Sinanju and his ungrateful pupil who drops magazines. Not a word," Chiun said. "Wait until I start writing for this magazine. Then you'll see its quality improve," he said.

Remo looked out the window at the park.

Could the assassins have been hired by Wimpler? That made no sense. He sounded as if he liked to do his own killing.

The night was moonless. The park would be perfect for an invisible assassin.

CHAPTER TWELVE

Elmo Wimpler entered Central Park near the East 72nd Street entrance a few minutes after 11 P.M.

Dressed in a white shirt and slacks and carrying a paper bag, Wimpler had as much chance of survival walking through the park as a piece of sirloin thrown into a cage of starving Dobermans.

But only seventy-five feet in the park, Wimpler darted from the pathway and into a cluster of bushes. He congratulated himself on being unseen.

But Wimpler was wrong.

He had been seen by Bats Agron. Bats was lounging against a pipefence, fingering the switchblade knife in his pocket and when he saw Wimpler enter the park, he wrapped around himself the dark cape which had given him his nickname and slid back in the shadows to watch. The little man in the white shirt had victim written all over him, and Agron had smiled as the man walked ever closer to him.

Then the little man had run into a clump of bushes. Probably some kind of fagola, Agron thought. Well, he might have been waiting to meet his boyfriend, but he was in for a surprise. He was going to meet Bats Agron.

The slim, smooth-faced, Latin youth took his knife from his pocket and held it in his right hand, his finger on the switch that flipped it open. He walked through the splash of sparse bushes into a small clearing, then looked around. It was a dark night, but that white-shirted man should have stood out like a lighthouse. Agron looked all around him, but saw no one.

"Shit," he cursed softly to himself.

"Looking for someone?" came a soft voice. It seemed to come from behind Agron's right shoulder. He turned, but saw nothing, just another silhouette of just another bush. He turned in the other direction, straining his eyes to see into the darkness.

He never had a chance to press the switch on his knife. He felt something metallic pressing against both sides of his head, then he heard a voice say, "So long, sucker," and then there was a flash of pain.

And then nothing.

Elmo Wimpler was pleased. He wiped off the skull-crusher and replaced it into the waistband he had designed to carry his equipment. Since leaving his house, he had been giving a lot of thought to the problem of his invisibility. He was invisible in total darkness, but in anything less than that, he was visible as a silhouette, without features, almost a shadow, but still the silhouette of a man. He had realized that his protection would be much greater if he could change his silhouette, and out of a few pieces of cardboard, hinged along their long edges, he had fashioned a folding screen, shaped roughly into the outline of a bush. He had painted it with his invisible, black paint also. In a dark park setting, he could just open the screen and anyone glancing in that direction would see nothing but the dark silhouette of just another bush, instead of the outline of a man.

He had wondered if it would work. The body of Bats Agron, lying at his feet, his skull in pieces, had just given him his successful road test. It worked.

Whistling lightly under his breath, Wimpler folded the screen under an arm and began strolling off toward the Sheep Meadow to meet the people who wanted him to kill the Emir of Bislami.

He knew little about the Emir, except what he had seen on the television newscasts. But politics didn't matter to him. What had mattered was that the people he had called were willing to pay a million dollars each for the Emir's death.

Wimpler still hadn't made up his mind. Should he kill the Emir and admit it to the world, challenging them to catch him? Or should he do it silently, as a professional, an anonymous hit man?

Why not? He could do both. He could take the credit for the Emir's death. People would be lining up to hire him. *Contract* magazine was filled with ads from people looking for killers. He could pick and choose.

But first, his two-million-dollar job.

He realized now how foolish he had been on the Brooklyn dock to have asked for so little to kill that federal witness. But that was then. The person who asked for that little amount was a wimp, and that wimp was dead. Alive now, in his place, was Elmo Wimpler, Elmo the Invisible Killer, Elmo the Scourge of the World.

He laughed aloud with happiness. From sheer joy, he took the light oscillating device from his pocket and aimed it at one of the streetlamps that lined the roadway through the park. He pressed the switch. The light sputtered and died.

He remembered "The Shadow" radio show. That's what he was, a modern-day Shadow, striking fear into the heart of men.

The first meeting was scheduled to be held in the southwest corner of the Sheep Meadow. Wimpler was there a few minutes before midnight and when he saw that the area was empty, he found himself a dark spot near some bushes, opened up his screen and propped it onto the ground. Then he sat behind it, his head out, able to see around the entire clearing. He had his compressor on the grass next to him.

His thoughts went back to the evening with his unwilling neighbor, Phyllis. She had not been all that he had thought she would be. Maybe being gagged and bound had inhibited her. But that was in the past too.

He had no need to rape. The women would come willingly, once he had the money. That's the way women were. All women. He thought of his mother who had cheated on his father for years, accusing the senior Wimpler of not being able to provide for her in any decent way.

Often she would come home wearing gifts other men had provided for her and so great was her contempt for her husband that she never even tried to explain the gifts away. Elmo never understood why his father had tolerated it and stayed with her, and when she was dying, he sat at her bedside, holding her hand, the devoted husband to the end.

As he, himself, grew up, Elmo was never treated kindly by women, because he was smaller and weaker than most men. He might still be smaller but there was no longer any weakness about Elmo Wimpler. The invisibility paint had changed all that. Women would flock to him and he would use them and humiliate them and then dump them.

He quickly checked his wristwatch, sliding it out from under his long black sleeve. Two minutes till midnight.

Soon.

He saw someone enter the edge of the meadow. Two men. The taller one was thin, dressed in black shirt and chinos. He had dark hair and his eyes were deepset. The man with him was an Oriental, dressed in some kind of yellow kimono. He had seen the two men before. As they stepped into the light, he remembered. He had seen them outside his old house in Brooklyn. They had gone in to question Phyllis. He remembered that the taller one had asked him a lot of questions.

Police? He hadn't asked and the man hadn't volunteered the answer. But what kind of cops wore kimonos? At any rate, they might be dangerous and he'd have to get rid of them before the person he was waiting to meet arrived. That these two men were here, after they had been nosing into Curt's death, meant that they knew more about Elmo Wimpler than was good for them.

He aimed his electronic light oscillator at the nearest of the overhead lights and it sizzled out. Quickly, he zapped another nine lights and the Sheep Meadow was in blackness.

Holding his bush-shaped screen in front of him, he moved through the darkness toward the two men, feeling secure and safe, beyond their reach, beyond the reach of the law.

He heard the tall one say, "Dark," as he sat on a bench.

"Especially for a pale piece of pig's ear who looks only with his eyes and not with his other senses." That made no sense to Wimpler. Stealthily, he moved around behind the two men. He would handle the taller one first.

He removed the compressor from his belt.

"I wonder if our friend is responsible for the doused lights."

"No," said the Oriental. "All the bulbs decided to burn out at the same time."

"They don't make things the way they used to," the taller man said.

"Including disciples and students," the Oriental said. "And bushes."

Bushes? Had Wimpler heard right? But they couldn't have seen him. He must have misunderstood what the small, yellow man had said. And why was he waiting? It was time to remove these two.

He was ten feet behind them, in the blackness. As he cocked the compressor, there was a small hiss as gas from a carbon-dioxide cylinder flooded the drum from which the skull-crusher got its power.

Elmo cocked it and stepped out from behind his cardboard bush and moved stealthily toward the two men. He extended the compressor to accommodate the taller man's head.

As he did, he was startled to see the Oriental's hand, moving through the darkness, reach behind his own head and grasp one of the arms of the compressor.

How could he have done that? The compressor was just as invisible as he was.

A coincidence, but one the old man would pay for. He would be minus his fingers.

Wimpler pulled the trigger, releasing the trapped compressed air, but the arms of the compressor did not move.

A malfunction.

Impossible.

He pulled the trigger again, but again the arms of the crusher did not work. Then there was a strange ripping sound as the inner workings of the machinery rebelled against not being able to do what they were built to do and they ruptured.

Wimpler dropped the compressor and ran back toward the safety of his ersatz bush. He heard the men stand at the bench, and suddenly he feared that he would not be safe, even behind the bush, even cloaked in invisibility in this blackness.

"That way," he heard the Oriental say.

The two men were coming toward him. He peered out from behind the bush. Then he heard the sound and saw its cause. Fifty yards across the Sheep Meadow, eight men were racing toward them. They were carrying knives. Several of them waved them over their heads.

The taller man and the Oriental turned to look and Elmo scrambled away from behind his bush, running hard, back into the deeper darkness of the night.

When he was fifty yards away, hidden in the shadow of a tree, he turned. What he saw made his blood chill inside his body. The eight men with knives had surrounded the Oriental and the American with the hard face.

There was a sudden flurry of activity and then three of the armed men were down and motionless. For some reason, Wimpler knew they were dead, although he had not seen the tall man and the Oriental do anything.

He watched again. The five remaining men moved in, all attacking at the same time. Then two more of them were down. And Wimpler still had not seen the two potential victims move.

The three attackers who remained paused for a moment. This time, Wimpler was sure that the taller man did not move at all. He thought he caught a slight touch of movement on the part of the Oriental, and then three more men were down and the only ones left standing were the Oriental and his companion.

Wimpler didn't wait. He turned and ran as fast as he could deep into the park. He would not stop until he came out the other side.

Those two were far more dangerous than he could ever have imagined.

He hated them. For they had, this night, brought back the wimp, even if only for a few moments.

They had destroyed his compressor and worse, his sense of invulnerability.

He thought about it as he ran. It must have been luck. The Oriental could not have seen him. He had not even been looking in Wimpler's direction.

Elmo was still an invisible man, and he would respond as the new Elmo Wimpler.

With hatred and with power.

He hated those two men, the tall-thin one and the

old Oriental. They would pay for what they had done tonight to mess up his plan. He had two contracts scheduled and now both were gone.

He would devise a new skull-crusher. The two men might even have done him a favor exposing the malfunction in his weapon. But they had not done themselves a favor.

They had done themselves great harm.

They had put themselves at the top of Elmo Wimpler's must-kill list.

He continued running. He had another meeting scheduled.

CHAPTER THIRTEEN

Chiun looked down at the dead bodies surrounding them. Remo's head was in the air as if sniffing. He returned to Chiun.

"I know," Chiun said. "He's gone."

"You let him get away," Remo said. "You knew he was there and you let him get away. Didn't you?"

"A terrible error of judgment," Chiun said.

Remo had picked up one of the knives from the eight dead men on the ground. He felt the bone and leather handle. "It doesn't look like an American knife," he said.

"It cannot be," Chiun said. "The handle has not yet fallen off."

"I wonder who sent these clowns," Remo asked.

"And the other two back at that house. It seems we are not only hunters but hunted."

"Yeah," said Remo. "But you tell Smith you let Wimpler get away. You tell him."

Chiun touched his arm. Remo looked across the Sheep Meadow and saw a woman coming toward them. He recognized the hair and the walk even before he focused on the face.

Princess Sarra.

She was wearing a purple, silk blouse, jeans, high boots, and a headband that matched the blouse.

She also had a gun at her side.

She approached the two of them, watching them with suspicion.

"Princess," Remo said.

"Do not approach me," she said, pointing the gun toward him.

"You generally stroll around Central Park after midnight?" Remo asked.

"I was supposed to meet someone here."

"Who?"

"Someone who answered an ad I placed . . ."

"In *Contract* magazine," Remo suggested.

Her eyes widened. "How did you know that?"

"Because we did the same thing."

"And these things . . ." she pointed her gun toward the dead men ". . . these were what you met?"

"I don't think so. I thought maybe you could tell me who they are," Remo said.

"And how would I know?" she asked.

"Because it's just a little much of a coincidence that someone sends eight goons to kill us and then you show up. Checking up on their work?"

"Don't be preposterous," she snapped indignantly. "If I had sent someone to kill you, you would be dead."

"Then put the gun away," Remo said.

She looked at the pistol in her hand as if she had just realized it was there. She lowered it slowly.

"I'm sorry. I didn't know who I would meet here. It seemed to me the only way to help my brother."

"So you placed an ad. That was a chancy thing to do, Princess. Did you come alone?"

"No. Pakir stopped by my apartment just as I was leaving. He insisted on coming with me."

"Where is he then?" Remo asked.

"I made him wait in the car."

"You're a brave lady," Remo said.

"I am devoted to my brother."

"Then look at the faces of these men and see if you recognize them."

In the dark, the Princess had to stoop to look at the corpses. She carefully looked at each one. Then she stood up.

"I do not know any of them."

"Thank you," Remo said. "I know it wasn't pleasant."

"You killed so many, just the two of you."

"They were poorly trained," Remo assured her.

They looked up to see Perce Pakir approaching.

If he was surprised to see Remo and Chiun there, he did not show it. He ignored the two men.

"Princess, you are not hurt?"

"I am not."

"Good. Did you accomplish what you set out to do?"

"No, Pakir."

He pointed at the bodies. "Who are these people?"

"They set upon our two friends here and were vanquished," Princess Sarra said.

Pakir stroked his beard and surveyed the bodies of the eight men. He was clad in a simple business suit, but the ruby rings that adorned his fingers showed that this was no ordinary businessman.

"I commend you," he said to Remo, bowing slightly. To the Princess, he said, "I think, perhaps, we should be getting back. Remember I warned against this action."

"Pakir, I would advise you not to use that tone with me," she said coldly.

"I mean no disrespect, but it is dangerous here in this park as is well known. I want you removed to safety."

The Princess ignored him and turned back to Remo. "Do you think these men have any connection with my brother?"

"I can't say," Remo answered. "What do you know about the person you were supposed to meet here tonight?"

"Nothing. My advertisement was answered. I was told to put a telephone number in the *New York Times* where I could be reached. I was called by a man. He told me to be here tonight. At twelve-thirty."

"Thank you," Remo said. "My pleasure, Princess, as always."

"And it will be again," she said softly, and nodded to Chiun before she turned to walk toward the park exit.

Pakir nodded to Remo and Chiun, then ran after the Princess.

"I do not like that man," Chiun said.

"You've got lots of company," Remo said.

Remo watched Sarra and Pakir walk away until they were out of sight. She walked nice.

"Let's go, Chiun."

"Not yet. There is one more thing."

"What is that?"

Chiun turned and walked back to the bench where they were sitting. Step by step, he moved more into the darkness, out of the reach of the lights on the far side of the field.

Remo watched the old Korean as he stopped, bent over, and felt the ground. He straightened up. He had an object in his hands, a small box with two arms extended from it like crab claws.

It was painted in that invisible, midnight black, and as Chiun brought it back, Remo thought how eerie it was that even close up, he could see only the silhouette of the gadget. All the light that hit the center of the object was totally absorbed and reflected nothing to the eye.

"What is that, Chiun?"

"I believe it is your skull-crusher," Chiun said.

"Where'd you get it?"

"It was supposed to have made mush out of your worthless head, thereby making the outside identical to the inside," Chiun said.

"What do you mean?" Remo asked.

"Our invisible man had this around your head when I took it from him," Chiun said.

"He did?"

"Why must I tell you everything twice?" Chiun asked. "Yes, he did."

"And that's why you let him go? You were busy saving my life?"

"Actually, that was not on my mind," Chiun said. "I just thought this might be a valuable invention and worth saving for the world. Unlike some things, which are not worth saving at all."

"Little Father," said Remo.

"Yes."

"Thank you."

"You're welcome. You tell Smith that the invisible man got away."

CHAPTER FOURTEEN

"You let him get away." Smith's voice was cold as a New Hampshire ski slope on a winter midnight.

"Well, actually, I didn't see him," Remo said.

"Then how do you know he showed up?" Smith asked.

"Well, actually, he tried to crush my skull!" Remo said.

"Was he successful?" Smith asked.

"That's not funny, Smitty."

"Neither is letting him get away," Smith said. "I just don't know how you managed to pull that off."

"All right. If you want to know. He showed up. I didn't see him. He tried to kill me. Chiun could have caught him or saved my life. He decided to save my life. I happen to think he made the right decision."

"I'll have to think about it," Smith said. "No identification on those eight men?"

"None. And the Princess Sarra didn't know them."

"You believe her?"

"Yes," Remo said.

"He lusts after her," Chiun called out from across the hotel room.

"What did Chiun say?" Smith asked.

"He said if he had it all to do over again, he'd save my life again," Remo said.

Smith let it pass. "What are you going to do now?"

"I'm going to check out *Contract* magazine," Remo said. "You placed an ad and the Princess says she placed an ad. I'm going to find out who placed the other ad and see if that'll lead me to Wimpler."

"Do you think he'll still be interested in killing the Emir?" Smith asked.

"Yes. I think it's not just money with him," Remo said. "I've met him, I told you. And I think he's into power. He can't let us stop him from killing the Emir, or his whole idea of his own power goes down the tube. He'll try again."

"Interesting theory," Smith said.

"Everything's theory until you find out if it works," Remo said.

"Don't make me chase you down," Smith said. "Keep in touch."

Remo hung up. When he turned to Chiun, the old man was shaking his head. He looked up from his copy of *Contract*. "These articles are terrible," he said.

"What's wrong with them?"

"All they talk about is money and guns. What about the beauty of a perfect assassination? What about the tradition and the history and the glory of the art? This is written by Philistines for Philistines."

"I know. And you can do better."

"Who knows better than I?" Chiun said. "So when you go to the offices of these people, find out the name of their editor. You will need it when I finish my story for them."

"What's your story going to be about?"

"A civilized assassin in a world of nincompoops. I will call it 'Chiun Among the Barbarians.' "

"Smitty will love it," Remo said.

"He can do what he likes," Chiun said, "but I am not cutting him in. It is bad enough I have to pay you two percent."

"I thought it was three."

"Don't quibble about a few dollars, Remo. It is not seemly."

Remo found the office of *Contract* in a rundown building on East 23rd Street between Madison Avenue and Park Avenue South.

The office was on the ninth floor of the building, and giant, silver letters on the wall next to their door blared out the magazine's name.

But inside, the office was small and shabby. There was a man sitting behind the reception desk who looked as if his only purpose in life was to bite the legs off visitors.

"Yeah?" he growled as Remo entered.

"Is that any way to greet a man who's going to save your life?"

"Yeah? How you going to save my life?"

"Maybe by changing my mind," Remo said, "and not doing to you what you obviously deserve."

"Yeah?"

Remo was beginning to wonder if that was about it for his functional vocabulary.

"I want to look through your records."

"What for?"

"I want to know the names of your advertisers and which ads have been answered recently."

"Take a hike. Our records are private," the man said.

"How many other people work here?"

"Why do you want to know?"

"Because if there's anybody else here, I don't need you and I can shove you into your desk drawer," Remo said.

"Yeah?"

"Don't start that again," Remo said.

The man stood up behind the desk. He was six-foot-six and outweighed Remo by half a ton.

"There ain't nobody else here right now," he said with a sneer. "So it's just me and you, pal."

He extended a hand toward Remo like a wrestler offering a handlock test of strength.

Remo shrugged. It was better than killing him. Even with a busted hand he could still talk.

Remo joined his right hand to the giant's left. He exerted no pressure.

"If that's all you got, pal, you're in big trouble," the big man said. Slowly, he began to put pressure on Remo's hand. Remo neither flinched nor moved.

The giant frowned. "Playtime's over, buddy," he said. He exerted what he thought was enough pressure to crush Remo's hand and drive him to his knees.

Remo didn't move.

The big man blinked and his forehead was now a map of lines and creases.

"I'm right handed," he complained.

Remo nodded. They unlocked hands, then locked again, this time with Remo's left against the giant's right.

The big man instantly turned on maximum pressure, every bit of energy and strength he could muster.

Remo didn't move.

Just as Remo decided he would have to crush the man's handbones into paste, the giant disengaged his fingers from Remo's.

"All right," he said. "You win. How'd you do that?"

"Training and clean living."

"Look, no offense, but you don't look like you train much."

"It's not that kind of training. It's all done in your head. What's your name?"

"Hal Barden."

"You the editor?"

"No. I'm everything but. This is just a two-man sheet. Mark Simons is the editor. He's inside."

"You were fibbing me," Remo said. "Naughty, naughty."

"I'm still here, so maybe it didn't work out so bad," Barden said. "Come on, I'll take you to the editor."

Inside the front office was another small cluttered office with another man sitting behind a small cluttered desk, wielding scissors and paste on some yellowed newspaper clippings.

"Mark, this is a friend of mine." Remo stepped forward.

"Remo Williams," he said, extending his hand.

"Yeah, yeah," said Mark Simons, ignoring the extended hand.

Remo looked at Barden who shrugged.

"Remo's interested in the magazine, Mark. I told him I'd show him around."

"Go ahead," Simons said.

"You ever buy manuscripts?" Remo asked Simons.

"Sometimes. If they're really good. You a writer?"

"No. But a friend of mine is," said Remo.

"He know anything about assassinations and contract killings?"

"A little," Remo said.

"Good. Send in anything he's got. Most of the people who send us stuff have been pulling their pudding for too long. They're like writing *Alice in Wonderland*."

"Thanks. I will."

Barden led Remo away. "C'mon. Another room back here."

He led him into another small room that appeared to hold all of *Contract's* files.

Barden waved toward a file cabinet. "That's our ad files. What do you need?"

"I need your ads on killing the Emir of Bislami," Remo said.

Barden nodded. "Yeah. He was hot in last month's issue. We had a couple on him."

"Three," Remo said. "Can you find them?"

"Sure." The big man opened the top drawer of the file cabinet and began riffling through envelopes.

"Do you keep a record of who answers?" Remo asked.

"No," Barden said over his shoulder. "We just forward them to the advertiser. We don't even open them. That way, we stay out of trouble with the law.

Here they are." He turned and handed Remo a slim manila folder.

It contained the copy for three advertisements and each had the name and address of the advertiser.

The first ad, "Ice an Emir," was inserted by a John Brown with a post office box in Rye, New York. That would be Smith, Remo realized.

The second ad was "Send a Monarch to the Mortuary." The ad form announced that it had been placed by Mrs. Jane Smith, with a New York post office box.

Remo handed it to Barden. "You remember anything about this ad?"

Barden looked at it. "Mrs. Jane Smith," he said. "Boy, do I. Tall, good-looking woman with great red hair. Spoke very elegantly. Like a queen she was."

That would be Princess Sarra, Remo realized. He looked at Barden with heightened respect. The man had sensed the innate royalty in the Princess, even when she was parading around as Mrs. Jane Smith.

The third advertisement was "Ever Kill an Emir? Check Out the Price." The record showed it had been placed, and paid for in cash, by a Mr. Riggs who lived in the East Seventies.

Remo jotted the name and address down on a piece of paper.

"I appreciate your help, Hal," he said.

"Any time. Maybe if you come back, you can tell me about your training."

"Even better," Remo said. "I might bring back my trainer with me."

"That'd be great," Barden said.

"Wait until you meet him," Remo said.

As he went to the door, Barden handed him the latest copy of *Contract*. "Here. A freebie."

"Thanks a lot," Remo said. Chiun would be glad to get it.

After Remo left, Mark Simons came out of his office and hit Barden's desk with his fist.

"Who the hell was that?"

"Hey, he was cool, Mark. You wouldn't believe how strong that skinny guy is. Some special training and . . ."

"Who the hell was he and what did he want?"

"Take it easy," Barden said. "He just wanted to look at some of our ads."

"What ads?"

"The ones about killing the Emir."

"And you showed them to him?"

"I wasn't about to tell *him* no," Barden said.

"You're a moron, Hal," Simons said and went back to his office. He locked the door behind him.

CHAPTER FIFTEEN

The name on the doorbell was James Riggs.

Remo pushed his way through the locked downstairs door and walked up the steps to apartment 3-A.

When he opened the door, Remo said, "Mr. Riggs, I'm here in answer to your ad."

"How'd you get my name?" Riggs asked. The man was tall, white haired, with tired, reddened eyes.

"Does it matter?" Remo said.

"The job has been filled," Riggs said.

"I can fill it better," Remo told him.

"I doubt it," the man said, looking sharply at Remo.

"Don't doubt it," Remo said.

"Look. I'm sorry, but the ad has been filled to my satisfaction. Good-bye."

He slammed the door shut.

Remo took the doorknob in his hand and bent it down until it snapped off on his side. Inside, he could hear the other half of the doorknob fall onto the floor of the hallway. Remo hit the door with the heel of his hand and it flew open.

James Riggs was standing five feet inside the apartment looking at the broken door, then at Remo, with fright in his eyes.

"Well, as long as you're in anyway."

"Thank you," Remo said. "Who filled the ad?"

"I don't really think . . ."

"Good. I'm used to dealing with people who don't think." Remo closed the door and brushed past Riggs into the apartment.

"If you don't leave, I'll call the police."

"Fine. I'll just tell them I came here to answer your advertisement for a murderer."

Riggs winced as Remo said the word "murderer." Finally he walked to a bar in the corner of the chrome and glass living room and poured himself a water tumbler full of Scotch. He drank half of it, then said, "I don't know. It was just a voice."

"You better explain this."

"I got a letter answering the ad. It told me to put a phone number in the *Times*. I did. I got a phone call from a man who told me to meet him in the Sheep Meadow last night at 1 A.M. I left my apartment to walk over there just around 12:40. The street was dark. He was waiting for me in the street. I couldn't see him. We negotiated a fee."

"How much?"

"A hundred thousand dollars."

"To kill the Emir?"

Riggs finished his drink, even as he was shaking his head.

"I didn't want the Emir killed."

"That's what your ad said," Remo pointed out.

"I just put that on it to attract attention. I figured anyone who'd tackle the Emir would be willing to take on a simple job like I had in mind. It was just a thought."

"Who did you really want hit?" Remo asked.

Riggs hesitated. Remo stepped toward him.

"My business partner," Riggs said.

"What kind of business are you in?" Remo asked.

"Advertising."

"It figures," Remo said. He got the name and address of Riggs' partner and left. As he went through the door, Riggs was pouring himself another drink.

"Be sure to have this door fixed," Remo said. "There's a lot of crime in New York." Riggs didn't know how lucky he was. If he had been in any business but advertising, Remo might have extracted a price for his trying to have his partner killed. But Remo did not think there should be any law against killing advertising men.

He walked down the stairs and on the first landing met Princess Sarra coming up.

"We seem to be covering a lot of the same ground," Remo said. "No Pakir today?"

"I do not need an escort everywhere I go," she informed him. "Mr. Schwartzenegger."

"Call me Remo," he said.

"They told me at the magazine that you had been there," she said.

"No point in covering the same ground twice. Come with me and I'll tell you what Riggs had to say."

She considered it.

"Are you suggesting we work together?"

"We are on the same side, aren't we?" Remo asked.

"I know what side I am on, Remo. Is that your side?"

"Yes," he said.

"Then let us go to my apartment and talk," she offered.

"All right. But we have a stop to make first," Remo said as he took her arm and walked her back down the stairs.

"Where?"

He told her what Riggs had just told him.

"We are going to warn his partner?"

"No. He's in advertising," Remo said. "But I want to see if Wimpler's been there yet. If not, maybe we'll just hang around for a while."

A taxi brought them to an apartment building almost identical to the one they had just left, except it was on New York's West Side, on the other side of Central Park. Remo checked the mailboxes, forced the door and they rode the elevator to the ninth floor.

The door was open.

"Stay behind me," Remo told the Princess.

"How gallant," she said, but Remo could hear the tension in her voice. She was frightened. Somehow it made her seem warmer and even more desirable.

The apartment did not appear to be ransacked. There was no sign of a struggle. Remo left her in the living room with orders to stay put while he looked around.

The bedroom was dark as Remo pushed open the door. Heavy drapes sealed out all light from outdoors. Remo remembered how close he had been to death last night, and he paused, heightening his senses, listening to hear if an invisible Wimpler was still in the room, ready to smack him over the skull with an invisible baseball bat.

But there was no sound from the room.

Remo went in.

The body of Riggs' partner was on the floor. He

had apparently been undressing when Wimpler struck. He was wearing socks and underwear. His shirt and suit were tossed over the back of a chair. Next to him was a portable TV set with a cracked screen.

Remo heard a sharp intake of breath behind him. Sarra had followed him into the bedroom and seen the body. The back of her right hand was pressed up against her mouth; her eyes were opened wide; her left hand against her breasts completed the classic pose.

"Don't scream," he ordered.

"I do not scream," she told him as she dropped her hands to her side.

Remo bent over the body to examine it. His head had been crushed, but not with any special device. Apparently Wimpler had knocked the man unconscious, then dropped the television set on his head to make sure of death.

Advertising had scored again. Riggs' partner was dead. The death was just a little more direct and quick than that usually inflicted on Americans by advertising.

"Let's go," Remo told Sarra, touching her elbow and turning her around. "Don't touch anything."

"Shouldn't you call the police?" she asked.

"No."

They rode the elevator down and found a cab cruising past on the corner.

Sarra gave the driver the address of her apartment.

At her penthouse, overlooking the East River, she offered Remo a drink which he declined. It had been years since he had tasted liquor and the

115

thought of drinking alcohol, a substance used to dilute lacquer, made him feel sick.

She did not make one for herself. She sat on the couch next to him, drew her long legs up beneath her and asked, "What did that all mean to you?"

"That dead guy?"

"Yes."

"Only that I missed a chance at Wimpler."

"That's all?"

He shrugged. "I'm sorry if that disappoints you, Sarra, but he didn't mean anything to me."

He could see that his viewpoint didn't disappoint her. It might even have excited her because she moved closer to Remo on the sofa.

"Do you think this man Wimpler will try to kill my brother?"

"Yes."

"Why? Who would he work for? What has he to gain?"

"You're right there. He doesn't have a contract. He didn't get one from us and he didn't get one from you. The other advertisement was a phony. But the fact is that your brother is a wanted man and the price on his head is very high. It won't be hard for a man, especially an invisible man, to make contact with somebody who'll pay him a lot of money to kill your brother."

She nodded. "I don't know why," she said, "but I have a feeling that he would do it even if there were no money involved."

Remo agreed. "We're talking about a man who was a pussycat all his life. Now he's got power, and last night Chiun and I challenged that power. I don't think he can ignore the Emir. Otherwise it tears down all he's tried to do with himself. I don't think he can resist the challenge."

"And you?"

"What about me?" he asked.

She touched his arm, then his cheek and finally his lips. Her fingers were cool and smooth as they traced the outline of his mouth.

"Can you resist a challenge?"

"Only when I want to, Princess," said Remo.

And this time he didn't want to.

It was almost midnight when Remo left Princess Sarra's penthouse apartment and her bed.

As he rode down in the elevator, he felt oddly satisfied with himself and began to analyze the feeling. For a long time, he had been able to satisfy any woman. He was like a machine, not getting personally involved, just doing a job. All the result of 27 steps taught to him by Chiun.

Usually, Remo went down those steps with clinical detachment, stopping at whatever step was the most the woman could stand. The best was usually around step 13.

All neat and precise and mechanical. And boring.

While technique flowered, desire had shriveled to nothing.

But not this time.

It was not just Sarra who had enjoyed their marathon, he had, too. It had nothing to do with love either. Love was an emotion of weakness, an emotion he tried to restrict in himself, for he could afford no weaknesses. Falling in love would make him vulnerable, and a vulnerable man in this business was a dead man.

This had just been sheer rollicking physical joy. If he had been able to tell Chiun about it, Chiun would have thought it disgusting because it was sex without procreation as a goal. But there had been nothing disgusting about it. It had just been a celebration of life by two people who appreciated life. It had been happy. There was no other word for it.

Preoccupied by these thoughts, Remo strolled out of Sarra's building at precisely midnight.

CHAPTER SIXTEEN

Slits Wilson liked midnight in Manhattan. It was the time he usually did his best work.

He had earned his nickname with a knife, cutting slits in other people's bellies, and he was proud of it. He also earned his living with that knife and didn't live too badly, when he wasn't vacationing as a guest of the state.

But this was a chance to end those trips to jail forever. It was his big score, and if it came off all right, he would have enough money to set himself up with a couple of women. A couple of foxes working the street for him could really start pulling in the green. Then he could branch out. A little numbers business. Eventually, a little high class drug dealing.

But first this job. The dude wanted some other dude taken out, and there were five big ones in it for Slits. The dude told Slits to make sure he had enough help. Now, how many brothers would it take to ice one honkey?

But the man was paying and the man insisted, so Slits got hold of three others, and now they were waiting across from the big apartment house for one white dude to come marching out into their arms.

Willie the Whip was Slits' main backup man. He was the first one Slits thought of bringing in on this job. Willie wasn't bad with a knife, either, although

119

Slits thought his slambang technique lacked style. Willie was Slits' age, 26, but where Slits was short and stocky, Willie was tall and reed-thin.

Willie had volunteered his brother-in-law, Tailor Taylor. He got his nickname because when he wasn't mugging old ladies, he worked in a dry-cleaning store. Slits hoped that he wouldn't screw things up.

Number four man in the quartet was Big Louie. Louie was five-feet-nothing when he stretched, but he was the meanest, baddest thing Slits knew. Except for himself.

"You jus' do what I tell you, hear?" Slits instructed. "This just one guy, but the man say he a bad ass, so we gonna be careful."

"Gotcha."

"Raht."

"Cool."

"Now he gonna come out that door. Me and Willie be on up here, Louie and Tailor be down there. If he come this way, you come in behind him. If he go your way, me'n Willie be behind him. Dig?"

"Gotcha."

"Raht."

"Cool."

"Now I cuts him first, see, 'cause it be my job. Then he be yours. Make sure we gets his wallet so it look like he was took off. And then when we done, you gets a hundred each. Dig?"

"Gotcha."

"Raht."

"Cool."

"Take yo' positions," Slits said.

* * *

120

The carefully contrived plan, the high point of Slits Wilson's intellectual life, had one flaw.

It handled Remo if he turned left or if he turned right. But Remo came out of the apartment building and without pausing, walked directly across the street, leaving behind him four very confused young men.

As their leader, Slits knew he had to improvise, if this whole deal wasn't going to get out of hand.

He went running across the street toward Remo.

"Hey, hey. Stop. Hey, hey," he called.

Remo stopped and looked at him. He saw three other young men fall in and start crossing behind Slits.

"What do you want?" Remo asked.

"Got a match?" Slits said, thinking quickly.

"Where's your cigarette?" Remo asked.

Still thinking quickly, Slits said "I musta dropped it."

"Then you don't need a match."

"Dammit, honkey, I needs a light," Slits said. He was not about to be dissuaded from a good plan just because of some uncooperative honkey.

"Rub your head on the sidewalk," Remo said. "That should give off a spark."

Slits saw the other three coming up on them now so he whipped out his knife.

"I gonna cut you," he said.

The dude didn't even look scared. "Why don't you talk right?" he said. Then the dude's hand moved faster than he could follow and his blade was gone.

"Shit, mah blade. Willie!" he called.

Willie jumped forward, nervously waving the

121

blade in his hand. Suddenly, he felt something hit his hand and the blade cut a narrow furrow in Slits' cheek.

"Sheeeit," Slits yelled, grabbing his face. "You cut me, you turkey."

"It weren't my fault, Slits. Honest."

"Shut up and cut him!" Slits yelled. "You too!" he yelled toward Tailor and Louie.

Slits watched what happened next with wide eyes, not really believing it.

Tailor made a stabbing motion at the honkey and suddenly the honkey wasn't there. Tailor and his blade kept going until the blade buried itself to the hilt in Willie's stomach. Willie's scream cut through the silent midnight in Manhattan like an icepick piercing soft bread. While Tailor stared in horror at Willie's body slipping to the ground, Slits saw the honkey pick Tailor up and toss him head first through the windshield of a parked car.

Louie charged the dude from behind with his knife, but then the dude wasn't there. He was behind Louie. He tapped Louie on the shoulder and when Louie turned, the honkey jabbed him in the stomach. With his finger. Louie went down and Slits knew somehow, with a sinking feeling in his stomach, that Louie was never going to get up.

Where was his blade? Slits looked around the ground, anger overwhelming his good sense. Gonna cut that dude. Gonna cut him good.

Just as he got his hand around the hilt of his knife, he couldn't breathe. Something had him by the throat and he felt as if his throat had closed up tight. Then he saw the honkey's face in front of him, as if it were floating in a haze. The honkey was saying something, asking him a question.

"Who sent you?" the honkey was asking. Sheeeit, Slits thought. I don't even know nobody's name. Just a white guy.

He tried to say I don't know, but it came out like "Ahdun" and then he remembered the knife in his hand and he swung it around, but before it reached anything, the steel band around his throat tightened up even more, and he could feel his brain exploding, and he dropped the knife onto the sidewalk. And then fell to join it.

Remo looked down at the body. He hadn't really wanted to kill the man, but his reaction had been automatic. Also, Remo's reactions had been slow and he had been stupid.

Chiun was right as usual. Remo had allowed himself to be affected by a woman and it had altered his reactions.

He looked at the three men on the ground and at the still feet of the man stuck through the windshield. Just run-of-the-mill, New York thugs. Bag-grabbers and lady-beaters.

But who? And why?

He stepped back and looked up at the penthouse window of Princess Sarra, suspicions invading his mind.

Had she set him up?

A man watched the action from down the block. He shook his head. He had known they would screw it up.

He watched Remo walk toward him. He lounged against a car, lit a cigarette and waited.

When Remo was thirty feet away, he stepped away from the car, pulled out a pistol, took careful aim, and fired once.

And missed.

Impossible, he thought.

He fired again. He couldn't have missed at this range, but the man didn't even try to duck. He just kept coming straight on.

He fired four more times. The man was still coming toward him. He swung his gun at the man's head, but the man seemed to get out of the way of the blow without really moving.

Then Remo was on him. He felt hands on his throat. He snapped the knife out of its wrist spring. He jabbed at the man's eyes.

Remo slid below the blow, but then he heard the spine crack. Disgusted with himself, he let the man drop to the sidewalk.

Remo looked down at him. A white man. He bent down and felt the man's jacket pocket.

Good. A white man. With a full wallet. Remo took the wallet and started jogging back to his hotel room to tell Smith.

But his mind was still on Princess Sarra.

CHAPTER SEVENTEEN

"He was what?"

Smith repeated it. "I said, he was a federal agent until last week, when he quit."

"What's an agent—an ex-agent—doing trying to kill me?" Remo asked.

"I don't know. I hope you can find out," Smith said.

"All right. By the way, did Chiun speak to you?"

"No," Smith said. "Why?"

"Because he wasn't here when I got back," Remo said.

"He did not talk to me," Smith said.

After he hung up, Remo looked out over the city. An ex-agent. Was he, really? There wasn't anything simpler than having a guy quit first so that if he was caught trying to perform the job his bosses had sent him to do, they could always wash their hands of him. He quit. He wasn't working for us.

But for that to be the case, it meant that the United States government might be involved in trying to kill the Emir. It wouldn't surprise Remo. The country had had a solid tradition over the last five years of turning its back on its friends. Washington was known around the world as Hand-ups-ville. Nothing coming out of Washington anymore would surprise him, including trying to eliminate

125

the Emir just to solve the publicity problem of keeping him alive inside the United States.

Why not? It made as much sense as anything else. And where was Chiun anyway?

The taxi driver had not wanted to go all the way to Sandy Hook, New Jersey, particularly not for that creepy, old, Oriental guy that he just knew wasn't going to tip worth spit.

In his own nice, New York way, he had tried to hint this to the old Oriental.

"Naaah, ain't no fucking way I'm going to Sandy Hook, 'cause when I get there, you'll tip me shit, and I'll be bringing back an empty cab, so fuck off, buddy."

He had tried to drive off, just as he had driven off hundreds of other times from other potential passengers, particularly in the rain, when they were getting soaked but refused to pay double the meter price for their ride. The driver put the cab in drive gear and gave it gas.

And nothing happened.

The wheels were turning. He could swear they were turning because he could hear them spinning and he could even smell the scent of burning rubber. But the cab was not going anywhere, and there was the little gook, still standing next to the cab, his hand on the front passenger's door handle, his head inside the window, promising to tip the driver a whole dollar if he took him to Sandy Hook.

"I ain't goin' nowhere. Frigging cab won't go."

"I will fix it," the old Oriental in the blue robe said.

"Yeah? How?"

Chiun slid into the front seat next to the driver, and now when the driver gave it gas, the cab just drove off neatly, as sweet as you please. The driver looked at the old man. If he didn't know better, he would have sworn the old man was holding onto the cab and stopping it from moving. But, no. That couldn't be.

Chiun saw the driver look at him and he smiled over at him. "It will not be necessary for you to talk to me while you drive to Sandy Hook. I will even pay you the extra dollar if you do not make conversation. In fact, be silent and I will make it a dollar and twenty-five cents. I know this is a lot but I have been in America a long time and I understand the native customs."

The cabdriver started to say something about probably having to stop for gas on his way to Sandy Hook, but Chiun shushed him with a long-nailed finger pressed across the front of the driver's lips.

"No talk," Chiun said. "I have to think."

There was no more talk.

The fare to Sandy Hook was eighty-eight dollars and seventy cents. Insisting that the driver should think nothing of it, Chiun paid him with ninety dollars in American money which he took from an old, leather purse, secreted somewhere deep in the folds of his silken kimono. Chiun insisted that the driver keep the entire remaining dollar and thirty cents as his tip, even though only a dollar and a quarter had been promised.

"This is because I am the most generous of men," Chiun had explained. The driver had nodded. All he wanted to do was to go back home.

The owner of the small fishing boat did not want

to go out to the island off the Jersey coast. As he explained to the little Oriental man in the silken kimono, he had already made his final party run of the day, the fish weren't biting anyway, and it was a good day for him to go home, lie alongside his backyard pool, and drink beer.

He had not realized how weak, how defective, how really dishonorable this goal was until the old Oriental had taken one of his heavy-duty, deep-sea fishing rods, suitable for catching anything from shark and marlin to small whale, from its holder alongside the railing of the boat. The old man held the inch-thick rod in both hands.

And then snapped it, as if it were a bread stick.

He smiled again at the fishing boat captain.

The captain decided a run out to the island would be nice on a day like today, and five dollars . . . he was going to get a whole five dollars for himself? . . . oh, joy. He would be glad to wait at the island dock until the old Oriental gentleman was done and ready to come back.

When the boat docked at the island, Chiun put down the two broken pieces of fishing rod he had held all the way across the water on the trip and cautioned the captain not to leave until Chiun returned. "No matter how long it takes," he said.

The captain had looked at Chiun, then at the broken fishing pole, and agreed to wait.

As he stepped lightly off onto the dock, Chiun wondered why Remo was always complaining about how difficult it was to get around using public transportation. Chiun never had any trouble.

The two guards at the front door were a different matter, but they were functionaries and that was the

128

role of functionaries in the world, to stop busy people from doing the things that must be done.

They explained to Chiun that no one was allowed inside the house without proper identification; Chiun explained to them that it was necessary for him to talk to the Emir; and they explained that this was impossible. Clearly impossible.

Chiun left them lying by the side of the porch. If he had not been so delighted at the ease of finding a cab and a boat, and not in such a good mood, he might have hurt them seriously, but instead, he just put them to sleep temporarily.

As he did the guard outside the door to the Emir's bedroom.

When Chiun went in, the Emir was sitting up in bed. His face lit up as he saw the old Oriental.

"Ahh, my friend, you have not forgotten to come back and visit me."

"It is my pleasure, Your Highness," Chiun said.

"I am surprised my men did not tell me you were on the way up."

"They will tell you all about it when they awaken," Chiun said.

The Emir laughed. "They are not hurt?"

Chiun shook his head.

"They are good men," the Emir said.

Chiun corrected him. "Perhaps they are good-intentioned men. It is not the same thing, Your Highness."

The Emir nodded, seeming to think about Chiun's statement for a few moments.

"Is your companion, Remo, with you on this visit?" he said. He turned toward the left window in the room, and the slowly sinking sun splashed his face with orange light, erasing the pallor that approaching death had laid upon his features.

"No. And it is not a visit. I am here on a mission," Chiun said.

"Yes?"

"Do you trust the people around you?" Chiun asked.

"As much as I must," The Emir said.

"Your assistant?"

"Pakir? He's been with me for many years. Yes, I trust him."

"Your sister, the Princess?"

"She loves me. I think she would give her life to save mine," the Emir said.

Chiun looked at the dying monarch. How much, he wondered, should he tell him?

"There have been attempts on our lives in the last several days," Chiun said. "By people of your country."

"Did you get their names?"

"No. They had no identification," Chiun said.

"But you were sure they were of my country? You know, many nationalities look alike," the Emir said.

"That is true," said Chiun. "But few of them eat alike. The mouths of these men exuded the smell of parindor, the spice that is used in cooking your national dishes."

The Emir nodded. "Why would they try to kill you and not me? Assuming that I am the eventual target?" he asked.

"Perhaps they are waiting for the price to reach its highest level," Chiun said. "After we were attacked by these men, the Princess arrived. And later so did Pakir."

"Master Chiun, I appreciate your good intentions. But I trust those people wholeheartedly. If they were there, as you say and I have no doubt, then they were trying to save me from murderers and assassins so I can wait for my natural death. Oh yes, I know I am going to die. I am prepared for it. You saw it in your examination, did you not?"

Chiun nodded.

"We will do our best to see that you are allowed to die in your own way, with dignity," the Korean said.

"I have faith that you will," the Emir said. He paused a moment, then said, "Tell me. Why is it I have this feeling that you and I have met? Or that there is some feeling between us that goes back many years?"

"We have not met," Chiun said. "But our ancestors did many years ago."

"On a battlefield?" the Emir said.

"No. The House of Sinanju was retained to work for your royal house. The Master at that time did his task, but was not paid. If I could only keep you alive, I would send you a bill for the amount."

"And if I could stay alive, I would pay it gladly," the Emir said. "The House of Sinanju," he said softly. "Of course, I have heard of it, in the archives of our land. I thought it was just a myth, a legend."

"A legend," Chiun said. "But not a myth. I will leave now."

As he was at the bedroom door, the Emir called his name softly. When Chiun turned, the deposed

131

ruler said, "I trust not the Americans. They were once my friends, but now I think I am an embarrassment to them. I think they would like it better if I were dead. Once it was not like this," he said but his voice trailed off into the mists of memory, and sleep came over his tired body.

"You will not come to harm while I live," Chiun said. "Or there will be many who pay the debt of your death." But the Emir was not listening; he had lapsed into sleep.

"Where've you been?" Remo asked when Chiun returned to their hotel room.

"I must account for my whereabouts now like a school child?" Chiun said.

"No, I guess you don't," Remo said.

"I went to see the Emir."

"And?"

"I wanted to hear what he thought about his sister," Chiun said.

"What does he think about her?" Remo asked.

"He trusts her."

"And you don't?" Remo said.

"I only know that the lady is clever and strong-willed, and that she has blinded you so you fail to see beyond her skin."

"Well, maybe not after tonight," Remo said. Quickly, he told Chiun about the attempt on him as he was leaving Sarra's apartment building.

"That woman is always close when death arrives," Chiun said.

The telephone rang. It was Smith.

"Remo," he said, "I've been doing some thinking."

"So have I," Remo said. "If that guy who tried to hit me tonight was a federal agent, it might just mean that our government is involved in an attempt to put away the Emir. Now if you still want us to protect him, we will. But we might wind up killing a lot of our own. Do you want to chance it?"

"That's just what I was thinking about," Smith said. "So I checked it out again. The man who tried to kill you tonight, well, his identification was that of an FBI agent. But he wasn't the man. I had the fingerprints checked. He wasn't the real agent."

"Who was he?"

"I don't know, but he wasn't an FBI agent."

Something was nipping at Remo's mind and memory. "Listen," he said. "The real agent. Was he assigned to guard the Emir?"

"Yes. He had been before he quit," Smith said.

"All right. Now the guy who's in charge of that detail . . . what's his name . . . Randisi. What does he look like?" Remo asked.

"You saw him," Smith said. "You tell me."

"No. You check your files and find out what his description is. I'll wait."

Remo heard the telephone being laid down and he could hear the desk-top computer screen slide open. He could hear typewriter keys being depressed, and then a faint whir. A few moments later, Smith was back on the line.

"He's thirty-five, salt and pepper hair, brown eyes, six-foot-two, two-hundred pounds. A small scar alongside the right corner of his mouth."

Remo shook his head as he listened to the rest of the description.

"Swell," he said. "That's not the guy, Smitty."

"What do you mean?"

"That's not the man Chiun and I saw on the island. Somebody's brought in a ringer. For all we know, the real Randisi might be dead. Maybe the guy who tried to kill me tonight too."

There was silence on the other end of the line.

Then Smith said, "That means . . ."

"That means that every agent we have on that island could be a phony. They could be members of a hit squad to kill the Emir."

"But why haven't they done it by now?" Smith said.

Chiun called from across the room. "Perhaps they are waiting for the price to get high enough."

"They're probably waiting for the price to get high enough," Remo said, with a thank-you nod to Chiun.

"It could be," Smith said.

"It is," Remo said. "And it's that Pakir."

"Why him?"

"He's in charge of security on the island," Remo said. "He'd know if he was working with phony agents. He would have checked them out."

"I'll send a helicopter for you," Smith said. "It will be the fastest way to get there."

"Why don't you call the island?" Remo suggested.

"And talk to whom?" Smith said.

Remo thought a moment. "Try the Princess. Maybe she's there by now."

"And if she isn't?"

"We're on our way," Remo said. "And Smitty . . ."

"What?"

"If he's dead when we get there, don't try to pin this one on me."

CHAPTER EIGHTEEN

Elmo Wimpler sat huddled under a blanket in the rear of the twenty-foot-long speedboat that was anchored 700 yards off the ocean side of the Emir's New Jersey coastal island.

He looked forward to the next couple of hours.

He had money in the bank now, courtesy of that dead advertising man, and now he had a mission: to take care of the Emir and the two men, the American and the Oriental, who had almost captured him in Central Park.

They were associated with the Emir somehow; he was sure of that. So he would be most likely to find them here on the Emir's island hideaway. Elmo Wimpler had to repay them. It was that simple because while they lived, there was always the threat that there was someone in the world who was not afraid of Wimpler's power.

He sipped warm tea from a thermos and thought about the Emir of Bislami. The man had once had a whole country in the palm of his hand and now Wimpler had that man's life in *his* own hands. Just the thought sent chills through him. And, anyway, when he had killed the Emir, he was sure he would find somebody willing to pay their fair share of the cost. That magazine had said there was a bounty of as much as twenty million on the Emir's head. Some of that he would collect; he was sure of it.

* * *

In a third floor office in the island mansion, Perce Pakir put some notebooks into a wall safe, then locked the safe with a flourish. The time had come.

The Emir's health was failing. If Pakir did not move soon, he would miss out on the contracts he had agreed to accept.

The money was important, but it had been more than money, too. For years the Emir had treated Pakir as a loyal aide-de-camp, but that was all. Never as an equal. Never as a member of the royal family. Never as a friend. Always as a subject.

Enough of that. The monarchy of Bislami was dead. Done forever. It was time to scratch something from the ruins. Pakir was going to scratch out ten million dollars for guaranteeing that the holder of the throne never went back to his country to reclaim his ancient monarchy.

He had hatched the plan on the very day that he and the Emir and the Princess Sarra had fled the country, ahead of the onrushing revolutionary troops. Once they had gotten to this United States island, he had been able to convince the Emir that he should personally supervise security arrangements, coordinating with the United States government's agents. He had insisted that the U.S. agents live on the island as a security measure. Then, with the Emir's own Royal Guard securely under his command, Pakir had met each U.S. agent as he arrived, disposed of each one of them, and substituted his own men by bringing them in by boat, at night, when the Emir slept.

There were twenty men on the island now, Royal

137

Guard and U.S. agents. But the U.S. agents weren't really U.S. agents, the Royal Guard was loyal to Pakir, and it was time for him to dispose of the Emir.

The only person who was not included on his side was the Princess Sarra. He hoped he wouldn't have to have her killed, too. He had plans for her.

It would have all been done before this, but it had taken time for Pakir to make his arrangements with the new revolutionary government of Bislami.

And then that idiot magazine had run those advertisements seeking people to kill the Emir, and those two real U.S. agents had come to the island. These were the only loose ends.

He had tried to dispose of those agents, the American and the Oriental, and had failed. And he had tried to get rid of whoever it was who would take the contract to kill the Emir. He couldn't afford to have anyone else running around, charging their island, taking credit for assassinating the Emir. But he had not been able to contact that man to put him away.

So there was no more time to waste. Tonight was the night the job had to be done.

Once it was over, the fake U.S. agents would just simply disappear. The United States would have to talk to the world about the murder of the Emir and the disappearance of almost a dozen U.S. agents. The world wouldn't buy it. It would simply look to the world as if the United States had killed the Emir and then killed the men who actually pulled the trigger.

It would serve everybody's purposes. Pakir could collect for the assassination from the new revolutionary government of Bislami and from the Russians for both the death and the embarrassment of the United States.

And he . . . and perhaps the Princess Sarra if she decided to be reasonable . . . would live the lives of the very wealthy. Perhaps in South America. Or Switzerland. Or anywhere. There were very few doors, national or otherwise, that were not open to a man with ten million dollars.

It was time.

The Emir stirred in bed. He opened his eyes for a moment, then closed them again, trying to drift back into sleep. Sleep was all he had left. And then death. He was helpless now to affect his own fate. If the many groups with a price on his head did not get him, the cancer would.

It was probably best this way. Sarra could go on to live her life. His friends in the United States, even though they had abandoned him in his hour of need, would be rid of a national embarrassment.

And the Emir would be removed from pain.

It was probably best.

Princess Sarra stepped through the doorway into her brother's room. He slept peacefully, and she sat by the side of the bed, in a chair, waiting . . . for what? For him to die? She felt helpless and wondered why she had come. Was it because she had pleasured her body with Remo earlier that day, and now felt guilty about disporting herself while her brother was the target of both killers and disease?

* * *

The helicopter had landed them on the New Jersey shoreline and a power boat was waiting to speed them to the island.

As they alighted at the main dock, Remo observed: "No one around. They're supposed to have somebody on this dock to check visitors."

"Perhaps they were not expecting guests," Chiun said.

"And perhaps they are discussing what to do about these guests," Remo said.

Chiun nodded. They heard the sound simultaneously. Footsteps, someone running through the brush from the main house. When he broke out into the open, they saw who it was.

It was Randisi, the top federal agent on the island. Or the man who played the part of Randisi.

He ran up to them, apparently out of breath and somewhat wild-eyed. Remo ran through Smith's description again in his mind. Randisi, Smith said, was 35, six-foot-two, two hundred pounds, with salt and pepper hair. This man was almost 50, five-foot-eight, fat, with red hair.

"They've taken over the house," he gasped, grabbing Remo by the shoulders. "The Emir is in danger. You'd better hurry."

"You're Randisi?" Remo said.

"Yes."

"You're right," Remo told him. "We shouldn't waste any time. We should get right down to it."

"Right."

Remo reached out and touched the fake agent on the back of the neck, where the spinal column enters the skull and is the most vulnerable. It snapped and the man fell at his feet, dead.

Chiun was already moving to the house. Remo quickly got to his side. "If they sent him ahead with that phony warning, they're waiting for us to come running right up to the front of the house," he said.

Immediately, they circled off, through the brush, to come around to the rear of the large four-story mansion.

As they passed the side of the house, they saw three men with suits, armed with automatic rifles, crouched near the pathway leading to the front of the house.

"Quietly," Chiun warned.

Remo nodded. If the Emir was still alive, any sign that Remo and Chiun were coming to his rescue might mean his immediate death.

They cut back in behind the three men. When they were only two feet away, Remo pursed his lips and hissed.

"Psssssst."

The three men turned around. Remo and Chiun struck at the same time. Remo took the man on the right. Chiun handled the one in the middle and the one on the left. Without a sound, the life was crushed from their bodies.

"Four," Chiun said.

"Smith said there were twelve federal agents on the island. And we saw eight Royal Guards. There's at least twenty," Remo said. He looked up, then hissed to Chiun: "There's two up on the roof. I'll go up and work my way down. You start down here and work up. One of us'll get to the Emir before they have a chance to kill him."

Remo went to the rear of the house. The building was brick and the thin indentation of mortar be-

141

tween the old, red bricks was enough for him to get finger and toe holds as he started up.

He went up the side of the building like an upside down film of a drop of rain running down a window. The secret was in the pressure; the body had to keep the pressure concentrated inward, into the center of the stone, and if the pressure were strong enough and concentrated enough, it overpowered the normal pull of gravity that would yank someone back down to the ground.

As Remo went over the top of the roof, he saw the two men, members of the Royal Guard, looking over the front brick wall toward the ground.

It would have been easy to throw them over.

Easy but noisy. And silence was everything now, if they were to keep the Emir alive.

When he was behind them, he tapped both men on their shoulders. They turned. In a blink of an eye, both dropped to the roof. Remo caught their rifles before they hit the rooftop with a clatter, and carefully laid them down.

Six down. Depending on what Chiun was doing below.

An unlocked trap door opened to the floor below. Remo dropped through it, right into the middle of two more guardsmen who were holding a ladder, getting ready to climb up to the roof.

The men looked at Remo for a split-second before reacting. It was a split-second too long.

Eight down. Remo caught the ladder before it hit.

Remo was alone on the fourth floor. Two floors down was the Emir's bedroom. Remo wondered if Princess Sarra would be with her brother.

Chiun had started in the front door, just as four men had walked out of the house. Each of them carried an automatic rifle.

All any of them saw was the purple blur of Chiun's nighttime robe. When he was done, the four rifles were propped together in a military tripod in one corner of the porch. On the other corner were propped the four men in the identical fashion. They looked like a singing group on a Philadelphia street corner.

No one inside the house had heard a sound.

Remo eased his way down to the third floor. There were two men around the corner at the bottom of the steps. Remo heard them talking.

"I think Pakir's dreaming," said one, in a harsh American voice. "There's nobody here."

"Just you and me," said another American voice.

"And me," said Remo, stepping from around the corner.

The two Americans wheeled toward him, their hands reaching for the guns in holsters on their hips.

Ten. That he knew of.

Inside the front door of the house, Chiun had paused, listening. There were no voices, no footsteps. The steps to the second floor were a long, curved staircase, and from the bottom floor it was impossible to see the second landing. On the side of the wall was the lightswitch, and Chiun threw it, casting the downstairs floor and the stairway into darkness.

"Light went off," he heard a voice from upstairs call.

"Check it out," another said.

"Sure. Anything's better than standing here."

Chiun moved to the stairway, and raced half up, stopping halfway to the next floor. He could tell by the sounds of their feet that two men were coming down. As they turned the corner so their vision covered the first floor, Chiun stepped out from the shadow at the side of the stairs. His long-nailed hands shot forward from his kimono sleeves and fastened themselves around the throats of the two men. They struggled for a brief instant, trying first to free themselves, then to scream. They did neither. Slowly, Chiun let them drop to the soft, carpeted steps. He ran up the remaining steps to the second floor. Remo was coming down the steps from the third floor.

Perce Pakir was walking into the Emir's room. He carried a pistol in his hand.

Both Remo and Chiun saw him enter the room as they reached the second floor landing.

Four men, two on Remo's side, two on Chiun's side, also watched Pakir enter the room.

It was their last view of life. Remo and Chiun each moved behind their two men and silently throttled them. They released the men's bodies which sank softly to the Persian-carpeted hallway floor, then the two men, Master and disciple, ran down the hallway, meeting at the center door to the Emir's room.

"Took you long enough to get here," Remo said.

"At my age, one must avoid sudden movements," Chiun said lightly. "Quiet."

Remo was silent as Chiun listened at the door. He turned back to Remo.

"There are three of them. The Emir, the Princess, and Pakir. Pakir is nearest us," Chiun whispered.

"Then we might as well go in," Remo said.

Remo tossed himself at the door, just at the critical point where the heavy oak and the brass hinges were misbalanced, and as the door swung open and Pakir wheeled, gun in hand, Chiun came through the door over Remo's body, and with an elegant motion of a slippered toe kicked the gun from Pakir's hand. Before the bearded aide could go for it, Remo had him paralyzed, digging his fingers into the Bislamian's shoulder muscle.

"He was going to kill my brother," Princess Sarra said. She stood next to the Emir's bed, leaning over, as if ready to shield her monarch with her own body.

"I know," Remo said.

Chiun retrieved Pakir's gun from the floor and put it on the table, next to the Emir.

The old monarch's eyes were fiery with anger.

"Why, Pakir? Why?"

"Because you are going to die anyway. Because when you die I will still be hunted by your enemies. But if I kill you, they will no longer hunt me and I will be wealthy. Wealthy beyond my wildest dreams."

"Ten million dollars," Princess Sarra said to the Emir. "That is what is offered for you."

The Emir looked at her, then back at his once-trusted aide. "Wealthy beyond your wildest dreams? Your trouble, Pakir, is that you always dreamed small," the Emir said.

His hand darted out from his bed and picked up

145

the pistol Chiun had put on the end table. He brought his arm around and squeezed off a shot at Pakir. Remo felt the man grow limp in his hands and dropped him to the floor where he lay motionless.

"Good shot," he said. "I'm glad you didn't hit me."

"I apologize."

"That's all right. I would have dodged," Remo said.

"Not for that," the Emir said. "For using the gun. There was a day when I would have strangled this traitor with my bare hands. But now . . . I cannot." He looked toward Chiun.

The old Korean nodded. "Weapons take all the fun out of it," he said. Something seemed to catch his attention and he went to the Emir's large, bedroom window which looked out over the Atlantic Ocean.

He turned back to Remo.

"There is something out there," he said.

"A boat," Remo said.

Chiun nodded. "A black boat. Very black."

CHAPTER NINETEEN

Elmo Wimpler was almost ready to go.

The joke would be on the man he rented the boats from when they were found, painted black, and he wondered why someone would want to deface his boats.

The boats had taken more paint that Wimpler had expected and he was glad that he had made up a new batch of the invisibility paint and put it into spray cans. The paint job wasn't much, but it would do for a quick operation.

Maybe when this was over, and he found someone willing to pay him for having killed the Emir, he would move onto a boat. A yacht of his own. And he would only get off the ship when he wanted to make a contract for a killing, or to shop for supplies and food. He did not think he would leave the boat for a woman. It no longer interested him. He had thought a lot about women since the night he had worked his will on Phyllis and, frankly, there was no comparison. He preferred killing to sex.

And tonight he would kill his first monarch, he thought, as he finished pulling on his invisible, black trousers.

There were twenty-one dead men on the island, counting Pakir.

Remo called Smith to tell him that the Emir was all right.

"Everyone else is dead?"

"They were all fakes," Remo said.

"I hope so."

"They were. And the Royal Guards were in Pakir's pocket because they figured if they stayed loyal to the Emir, they'd be next on the hit parade."

"Have you seen any sign of the bodies of our real agents?"

"I'd have to guess that they were dumped out at sea," Remo said.

"The Princess?" asked Smith.

"She's well and she's clean. She's the only one on the island who wasn't part of it. I think Pakir had a thing for her and wanted to keep her alive."

"What are you doing now?"

"Chiun and I are going after Wimpler. His boat is out there offshore."

"Is that wise?" Smith said. "Leaving the Emir and the Princess alone?"

"It is now. I've taken care of it," Remo said.

"Be careful," said Smith.

Remo hung up the hall telephone and turned to find Sarra watching him from the doorway of her brother's room.

"The Emir?" Remo asked.

"Not well. Pakir's disloyalty is a crushing blow. Chiun is with him."

"You trusted Pakir too, didn't you?"

"I disliked him, but I didn't think he would turn on the Emir," she said.

"He had the hots for you," said Remo.

148

"The hots?" she asked.

"Slang. He lusted for you."

"Probably. But not I for him. I only have hots for you," she said.

"Thank you," Remo said. "It beats the hell out of love every time."

She stepped up and hugged him. "You will be careful with this other man you wait for?"

"Don't worry. You'll remember what I told you?"

"Yes. I do not understand it, and I do not believe it, but I will do it."

"Just do it," Remo said. They walked together to the doorway of the Emir's room.

Chiun was leaning over the thin and bony ruler who was speaking.

"Since I will die in any case, I would rather have been murdered than find out that Pakir, my friend, had plotted against me."

Chiun's face tightened with anger. "That is stupid," he said.

The Emir looked shocked.

"What?"

"Stupid, stupid," said Chiun. "You are giving to others and their actions the power of life and death over you. But if a man is to be a man, he must rule not only a country, but the circumstances of his life and the conditions of his death."

The Emir obviously thought about that for a moment, then nodded. "There should be no lament for traitors," he said.

"Are you all right, my brother?" Sarra asked as she entered the room.

"Just tired," the Emir said.

"Rest," she said. "I will sit with you."

"And he will be about his majesty's work," Chiun said.

From the doorway, Remo called to Sarra. "You know what to do?"

"Yes," she said. "I do not understand, but I will do it."

And even as Chiun and Remo were going down the stairs toward their waiting boat, Princess Sarra busied herself in the Emir's room, lighting candles. Candles taken from all over the house. She lit them on the dresser and near the windows and on the small end tables and desk and on the mantle.

As their boat powered away from the main dock, and turned behind the small island, Remo saw the flickering of candles in the Emir's room, and smiled to himself. Elmo Wimpler might have a device that could short-circuit lightbulbs, but it would take a lot of concentrated puffs of air to blow out all those candles. And while he was doing it, he would be just another little man in a black suit, and Princess Sarra, with Pakir's revolver, would blow him into pieces.

The Emir was safe.

As their boat moved quietly, slowly toward the dark silhouette against the dark, nighttime sky, Remo said to Chiun, "You are really fond of him, aren't you?"

"He was the holder of a great throne," Chiun said. "He has been replaced by jackals who have neither his courage nor his character. They will, in the sacred name of 'the people,' exalt mediocrity, stupidity, and brutality. I would have a monarchy every time."

"Why?" Remo asked. "Monarchies can be mediocre, stupid, and brutal too."

"But if they are, they can be changed with the disposal of one man. Because of this, the best monarchs know that they must rule with intelligence and compassion. This man was one of the best. The poor people of his nation will soon know how much of a man he was. Shhhhh. We approach."

Remo cut the engines. The boat continued drifting toward the larger boat, anchored some 40 yards ahead of them.

Elmo Wimpler had only taken a little while to decide with what weapon to replace his confiscated skull-crusher.

A knife.

An invisible knife which would, however, produce very visible blood.

He had treated three different knives with his paint, and fashioned a belt with large loops so he could wear them all on his waist. He would, when he had the time, practice throwing them. It would make him even more deadly, working in the dark, and without the telltale flash of flame that would give away his position if he used a gun.

He buckled his belt. It was time.

Time to ice an Emir.

He walked toward the front of the boat. And then he heard it.

A voice.

It was the American.

"Anybody home?" it called. "Ready or not, here we come."

They had felt themselves drift into the boat, but up close, without the boat outlined black against the sky, they could not see it. He and Chiun climbed out of their small boat, going up the side of Wimpler's craft, finding handholds and toeholds where none could be seen.

He couldn't believe his eyes. Climbing over the side of the boat, stepping onto the deck, were those two from the park. The American and the Oriental. They had found him.

Elmo Wimpler shrank back into the shadows, crouching down in a corner of the rear deck. He couldn't let them interfere. Not now. Not when he was so close.

He waited until they were both on deck. Then quietly he drew one of his knives. They began to walk about the boat when he noticed something.

Their feet made no sound as they walked.

But normal men should have made sounds as they walked around a wooden deck. Were they . . . something more than normal?

He put the thought out of his mind. He had no time. He had to get rid of them and get on to the Emir.

He stood up and took a step toward the American. And both men turned in his direction as if they had heard him.

He had made no sound. How had they known?

The Oriental pointed directly at him and said: "There?"

How could they know?

"It's all over, Elmo," the tall one said. "It's all over. Back to Wimpville for you."

No. No. Not now. Not ever.

He threw the invisible knife through the darkness of the night at the tall man, and the Oriental pushed the white man out of the way. Elmo watched as the knife struck the Oriental in the chest—hilt first.

Damn.

"A knife," the Oriental said. He saw the tall one nod. Elmo pulled another knife from his belt. Holding it in front of him, he charged the tall white man.

He didn't see the man's hand move, but something struck his wrist. The knife flew from his hand and over the side.

He rolled back away from the man and pulled his last knife from his belt. He stood perfectly still. If he did not move, they would have to come to him. And he was still the Shadow, the man who terrified other men, the man with the power of life and death over others.

"He's standing still, Chiun," the American said.

"He is right there," the old man said, pointing directly at Wimpler. "He has another knife."

"A piece of cake," Remo said.

Elmo tightened his grip on the knife and licked his lips. The Oriental moved closer to him on one side, the white man on the other.

Now. Within easy reach.

Wimpler swung the knife with all his power, aiming for the old man's skinny throat. But suddenly the old man wasn't there anymore.

"You can stop moving," said the Oriental into the

153

blackness. "But you cannot stop breathing, and we can always find you."

Blinded with anger and frustration, Elmo swung at the robed man with his knife again, feeling even more fury as he sharply expelled his air before the thrust.

The Oriental easily avoided the knife.

Then the tall one was behind him. Wimpler looked from one to the other, one to the other. He swung the invisible knife wildly around him. But his breath came in loud puffs and the men avoided the knife slashes. It couldn't be. The greatest invention of all time was being nullified by his own goddamned breathing.

He threw the knife at the white man. It missed as the tall man ducked and clattered harmlessly against the side of the boat.

.. He couldn't let himself be caught. He couldn't. They would ruin it all. Make him visible. Make him a nothing again.

He couldn't stand that.

Elmo Wimpler stood up straight and bolted to the rear railing of the boat.

"Chiun, the rail."

Wimpler jumped off.

The impulse to jump had been blind and suicidal, but without intending it or even thinking of it, Elmo landed in the little, electrically-powered, fishing boat he had been towing. He had planned to use it to motor silently into the Emir's island. As he landed in a heap in the boat, he felt a sharp pain in his ankle.

He started the electric trolling motor and tossed off the small rope that bound him to the bigger boat. Even this small boat had been treated with the invisibility paint and now they would never find him.

Remo sensed that Wimpler was jumping the rail. He was surprised when he heard a thud rather than a splash. He ran to the rail just as the electric motor started up. The son of a bitch had a small, invisible boat. Remo watched as the wake of the boat kicked up and it looked as if some giant, finned fish were swimming away from the larger boat.

"Chiun, he's got a boat. Let's get this thing started."

"Too slow," said Chiun. "He will be hidden in darkness by then. Swim."

Remo nodded and vaulted over the railing into the chilly, Atlantic water. He paused for a moment, then picked up the faint trail of the small boat's wake, slapping tiny pressure waves against his face. He straightened out his body atop the water and began stroking after the boat, making his body one with the water, letting the flow of the water surround his body and pull him with itself, stroking only to correct his direction.

Wimpler had looked back in time to see the tall man jump off the boat into the water. Was the fool actually going to try to catch him by swimming? Did he think he could outswim a motor-driven boat?

In disbelief, as he watched, the swimming man began to gain on him.

How could that be?

How could he swim faster than a boat?

And how could he see Elmo's boat to chase it?

155

He realized the answer to the second question. The man was following the wake of the boat and the faint sound of the electric motor. His invisible boat was doing him no good. It pinpointed his position beautifully.

Wimpler had to try to outrun the swimming man who, incredibly, seemed to be gaining speed but wasn't even stroking. He turned the boat's rudder, pushing it into a large, curved swing, a circle. Remo stayed close behind.

The circle closed tighter and tighter around the bigger boat.

Wimpler had a plan. He found a small aluminum oar under his seat. He turned the boat again. He glanced behind him. Remo was following tight behind his boat, only fifteen yards away.

This time, he turned the rudder of the boat sharply. The boat swerved inwards, and as Wimpler gave it maximum throttle it surged ahead, and raced straight on toward the larger boat. Wimpler waited a moment, correcting direction, aiming it at the large, black outline visible for a moment against the whitish clouds. Then he poised in the bow of his small boat. Suddenly, it rammed the bigger boat. Jarred, for a moment, Wimpler jumped up onto the deck of the larger boat, the oar raised over his head.

Chiun, in the corner of the deck, turned just as Wimpler raced for him, ready to swing the oar down atop the Oriental's skull. Then he would start up the large boat and race away from this swimming maniac who was following him.

Wimpler swung the metal oar at the Oriental's head. It struck something. But then, like a pole vaulter, Wimpler found himself thrown upward through the air, out into the ocean.

He was conscious when he hit the cold water. His instinct was to try to swim. He had gotten only three strokes when his arms began to tire and his legs to feel heavy. He began to sink.

Panic.

The clothing he had used to fashion his outfit became heavier as it absorbed water but his great invention—his invisibility paint—began to expand and to form bubbles which began filling up with water. It was swelling, becoming cumbersome. He felt the growing size of it pressing against his arms and legs, making movements difficult.

He opened his mouth to call for help but his mouth filled with water. He screamed, but it was only in his mind.

He tried to think.

Get rid of the clothes. Get them off.

He tried, but the garments seemed to cling to him like glue. His arms refused to move, to follow his commands to rip at his buttons and free themselves.

He felt as if he were wearing a suit of armor.

He felt numb.

He felt sleepy.

Then he didn't feel anything, anymore.

Remo hoisted himself up over the side of the larger boat.

"What are you doing?" Chiun demanded as he climbed back aboard.

"He crashed, Chiun. He rammed right into you. He probably sank like a stone."

"I know he sank like a stone, you white buffoon," Chiun said. "I threw him overboard. But his uniform. Do you realize we could make a fortune with that?"

"What?"

"Can't you see the possibilities?"

"I don't give a rat's ass about the possibilities," Remo said. "You're just money hungry."

"You do not want me to be rich. You want my people to forever starve, to be forever oppressed, to . . ."

Anything was better than listening to the whole spiel. Remo looked out at the calm sea. There was a faint, little whirlpool of ripples about fifteen feet from the boat. Remo wondered how deep the water was.

"Well, since I'm wet already," he said.

Chiun patted him on the back in encouragement.

Remo dove over the railing into the water. When he reached the spot of the ripples, he dove straight down. He could not gauge how deep he had gone, but he could feel the pressure of the surrounding water compressing the air in his lungs. And then before him, he saw Elmo Wimpler. The little man's eyes were open in the horror of death. No more bubbles came from his open mouth. His hair floated around his face like a gang of anarchistic snakes. He had reached the point in the water where the weight of his body matched the weight of the water surrounding him, and he hovered there, neither going up nor down. Some day, when the gases of death had formed inside his body, the specific density of the corpse would change, would lighten, and he would pop to the surface like a cork.

Remo reached out to touch the body and realized that the suit Wimpler was wearing had swollen like a balloon. His arms and legs looked as if they were welded together. The clothing was covered with great bubbles and even as Remo watched they broke open and disintegrated and slipped away into the water, tiny black slicks of paint breaking down.

He grabbed Wimpler by the neck and swam to the surface with Wimpler's body in tow. When he got to the boat he pushed the body up and over, onto the deck.

He followed.

"I can see him," Chiun complained.

"Not much of a looker, was he?" Remo said.

"The water has destroyed his secret," Chiun said. "Or the salt."

"Yeah," said Remo. "Something's ruining his cover."

"Throw him back," Chiun said.

"I beg your pardon," Remo said.

"I said throw him back. The suit is useless and he is dead so he is useless."

"Throw him back, like a fish?" Remo said.

"Just throw him back, like anything you want to throw him back as," Chiun said. "A fish, a stone, a pound of marbles. Throw him back and let us return to the island."

"Sheesh," Remo said. He hefted the body up, over the rail and dropped it.

It made a bigger splash striking the water than any too-small fish that had ever been thrown back.

The big boat lurched. Then Remo could feel it drop a few inches. He went to the other side and looked down. There was a gash in the wooden side.

159

The invisible paint had been ripped off and beneath it, Remo could see the torn wood, caused when Wimpler's small boat had slammed the side. The big boat was sinking.

Let it, Remo thought.

"Let's go," he called. "Time to go home." Chiun followed him into their small boat. They cut loose and turned back to shore, back to New Jersey, back to the Emir and Princess Sarra.

When they returned to the mansion, Remo called Smith from the first floor hall telephone.

"It's over," he said.

"Wimpler?"

"Dead. Bottom of the ocean."

"His invisible outfit?" Smith asked.

"You're getting just like Chiun," Remo said. "The salt water destroyed it."

"And the Emir?"

"Okay, the last time we looked," Remo said. "I guess they can relax for a while."

"Probably not," Smith said. "There will always be someone who wants him dead, Remo; someone else who will hire a hit man or a mercenary or a whole army. I'm going to send in new security forces tonight to guard him. You make sure that you don't leave there until everyone is in place."

"Okay, Smitty."

Remo hung up and looked over at Chiun who still seemed disconsolate.

"C'mon, Chiun. Cheer up. Let's go upstairs."

There was no answer to their knock on the Emir's door. They walked in to find the Emir lying on his back on bed, his arms flung out to his sides in a

160

grotesque parody of death. But this was no parody because there was no life left in the monarch's body. There was a smile on his face.

Princess Sarra was seated by the bed, her head in her arms. She was crying. Next to her on the mattress was the revolver with which she was to protect her brother. The candles still burned in the room.

'She looked up as Remo and Chiun entered.

"Remo . . ."

"I know."

"He died only moments ago. He was sleeping and then he just stopped breathing." She said it with a tone of desperation as if she expected Remo to be able to do something to repeal the Emir's action.

"His troubles are over," Remo said.

Chiun stood at the foot of the bed and bowed his head. "I salute you as a great ruler, a true son of a true throne."

The Emir was buried in the United States. The rulers of his country who had offered millions to have him back alive, so they could kill him, refused his body in death, and denied him burial in his native land.

Sitting at an outdoor cafe on University Place in New York, Smith asked Remo: "The Princess?"

"I put her on a plane."

"To where?"

"I didn't ask."

Chiun sat glumly at the little table, twisting a paper napkin into thread-thin strips.

Smith nodded toward him, his eyes asking Remo a question.

"He's been upset since we lost Wimpler's invisible paint," Remo said.

"Well, those samples you saved us and his car in the garage should give us enough to duplicate the formula," Smith said.

Chiun looked up sharply.

"And then what will you do with it?" he said.

Smith shrugged. "Turn it over to the defense department. Some kind of military application, I guess,"

Chiun went back to tearing his napkin, unhappy as he watched all possibility of commercial enterprise being drained from the invisible, black paint.

"Don't feel bad," Remo said. "In the wrong hands, that paint could have been used for a lot of bad things, Chiun."

"Name one."

"Well," said Remo. "It could have been used to paint Sinanju. Then Smitty's submarine, filled with gold, would never be able to find it."

Chiun said something sharply in Korean.

"What did he say?" Smith asked Remo.

"Trust me. You don't want to know."

"Try me."

"He said that when he's a world-famous writer, people won't treat him this way."

Special Preview

The mob couldn't kill him, the cops couldn't catch him, and even time can't slow him down!

NOLAN
by Max Collins

Introducing Nolan, a shrewd, restless tough guy with a talent for theft. A lifetime of heists under his belt and a bullet in his side have convinced him it's time to retire. Trouble is, an old enemy's blown his cover, and he can't touch a dime of his money without being busted. Robbed of his nest egg, Nolan's got to get out and hustle again . . . only now none of the old gang's willing to give him a hand.

Don't miss the Nolan *series,* coming in March from Pinnacle Books, wherever paperbacks are sold.*

The drizzle felt good on Nolan's face. The night air was chill, though not enough so to freeze the drizzle, and the light icy sting of it on his skin kept him alert as he waited.

He was sitting on a bench in the parklike strip of ground that separated the Mississippi River from the four-lane highway running along it. The highway connected the Siamese-twin cities of Davenport and Bettendorf, whose collective reflection on the river's choppy surface vied for attention with that of Rock Island and Moline on the other side.

Across the highway was where Werner lived.

Werner's home was a white, high-faced two-story structure, complete with row of six pillars, the rest of it having an aura of lush plainness that made it all the more obnoxious. Already bathed in light by the heavily traveled four-lane, the house was lit on right and left by two spotlights set on either side of its huge, sloping lawn, which banked down gradually to the highway's edge. Even through the heavy mist, the whiteness of the overlit house contrasted starkly with the moonless night around it.

Typical Werner logic, Nolan thought, picking a place like that one: status plus prestige equals respectability.

Nolan had been waiting just less an hour. His side of the road was darker, and the constant traffic flow and the hazy weather seemed likely to obscure him from anybody who might be on watch over at Werner's. He hadn't seen any watchdogs yet, but he knew one would show sooner or later—a Werner-style watchdog, two-legged-with-gun variety.

He smoked cigarette number one off the first pack of the evening, second of the day. He was pleased when the drizzle didn't put it out. Just as he was getting number two going, he spotted Werner's man.

The watchdog came around from the back, walking slowly around the house, probing the thick shrubbery on both sides of it with a long-shafted yellow-beam flashlight. He was slow and methodical with his search, and after the shrubs had been checked, he headed for the paved driveway to the left of the house. He stood at the far end of the drive and let the flash run down over it, then walked toward the back of the house again.

Probably a garage back there, Nolan thought, the drive leading around to it.

Three minutes later the watchdog reappeared at the right of the house and began to move slowly over the sprawling lawn, criss-crossing it half a dozen times before angling down to the highway's edge. He stood there for a moment in the light of a streetlamp, and Nolan got a look at him.

Not overly big, just a medium-sized guy, wearing a hip-length black brushed-leather coat that was open in front, revealing a dark, conservative suit, complete with thick-knotted striped tie. The man didn't look particularly menacing, but Nolan knew he'd probably been chosen for just that reason.

Subtle muscle. Typically Werner.

Nolan's hand in his jacket pocket squeezed down around the rough handle of the .38. He put on a smile and stood up from the bench. Stepping out into the stream of traffic, sidestepping cars, Nolan called out to the watchdog.

"Hey! Hey, buddy . . ."

The watchdog had turned to walk away, and Nolan met him about a third of the way up the sloping lawn.

"Say, I think I've gotten myself lost. You couldn't give me some directions, could you?"

The watchdog had a bored, bland face that didn't register many degrees change between glad, sad, and indifferent, though Nolan could read it well enough to rule out glad. The hand with the flash came up and filled Nolan's face with yellow light.

Nolan squirmed and held his free hand up defensively to shield his eyes, but he kept the smile plastered on. "Look, friend, I don't want to bother you or anything, I'm just a stranger here and got my bearings fouled up and thought maybe you could . . ."

"This isn't an information bureau," the watchdog said. "What this is is private property. So just turn your ass around and go back across the street and take off. Any direction'll do."

The flash blinked off, and Nolan could tell he'd been dismissed.

Nolan gave him a bewildered-tourist grin, shrugged his shoulders, and began to turn away. Before the turn was complete, Nolan swung gun-in-hand out of his pocket and smacked the .38 flat across the watchdog's left temple. The watchdog's eyes did a slot-machine roll, and Nolan caught him before he went down. Nolan drunk-walked the limp figure up the remainder of the lawn, carefully avoiding the glare of the spotlights, and took him over to the left side of the house, dumping him between two clumps of hedge. He checked the man's pockets for keys, but found none.

Subtle moves were fine for Werner and company, but right now Nolan hadn't the time or energy for that. He glanced out toward the highway, which by now seemed far away, and decided that there wouldn't be any threat from some public-spirited motorist stopping to question his handling of the watchdog situation. Thank God for mist and apathy.

He walked around the house in search of an unlocked window, trying not to let his out-in-the-open sloppiness with the watchdog bother him. He just didn't seem to have the patience to work things out smoothly these days. Making a mental promise to tighten himself back up, he tried the last of the windows.

Locked.

Well, there might be one open on the second floor, and a drainpipe was handy, but Nolan ruled that ap-

166

proach out: his side, while healing, was not yet in that kind of shape, and he was beginning to think it might never be.

He broke the glass in a window around the back of the house, seeing no need for caution since the neighboring houses on both sides were blocked by stone walls, and a large three-car garage obstructed the view from behind. A light was on in a window over the garage door, probably the watchdog's quarters, explaining the absence of house keys in the man's pockets. Nolan slipped his hand in through the glass-toothed opening in the window and unlocked it. Then he pushed it up and hauled himself slowly over and into the house.

He caught his breath. The room he found himself in was dark; after stumbling into a few things, he decided it was a dining room. A trail of light beckoned him to the hall, where he followed the light to its source, the hairline opening of a door.

Nolan looked in the crack and saw a small, compact study, walled by books. Werner was sitting at his desk, reading.

Several years had passed since Nolan had last seen the man, but their passing had done little to Werner: he'd been in his early twenties for twenty-some years now. The only mark of tough years past apparent in his youthful face was a tight mouth, crow-footed at its corners. The almost girlish turned-up nose and short-cut hair, like a butch but lying down, overshadowed the firm-set mouth. His hair's still jet black color may or may not have come out of a bottle, though Nolan felt fairly certain that the dark tan was honest, probably acquired in Miami.

A rush of air hit the back of Nolan's neck, and he started to turn, but an arm looped in under his chin and flexed tight against his Adam's apple, choking off all sound. He felt the iron finger of a revolver prod his spine as he was dragged backward, away from the cracked door.

A whisper said, "Not one peep."

The watchdog.

Shit.

"That gun in your hand," the whisper said. "Take it by two fingers and let it drop nice and gentle in your left-hand coat pocket."

Nolan followed instructions.

"Now," the whisper continued, "let's you and me turn around and walk back into the dining room, okay? Okay."

The watchdog kept his hold on Nolan's throat and walked him along, each step measured. Once they were out of the hall and into the dining room, the grip on Nolan's neck was lessened slightly, though the pressure of the gun was still insistent.

"Keep it quiet and you'll get out of here with your ass," the watchdog whispered. "I'm only going easy on you because I don't want my boss in there finding out I let somebody slip by me. A window with some busted glass I can explain; you in the house I can't. So just keep it down."

They approached the broken window through which Nolan had entered, and the watchdog released him, shoving him against the wall by the window. Enough light came in the window for the two men to make their first good appraisal of each other.

Nolan had been right about the guy being tougher than he looked. The whole upper left side of his face was showing a dark blue bruise, and a still-flowing trickle of red crossed down from his temple over his cheek, but the man's expression remained one of boredom, only now it was as though he were bored and maybe had a slight headache. He'd shed the leather topcoat, and his suit was a bit rumpled, although the striped tie was still firmly knotted and in place.

"Sonofabitch," the watchdog said, "an old man. I got taken down by an old man. Will you look at the gray hair. Sonofabitch."

Nolan said nothing.

The watchdog's upper lip curled ever so slightly; Nolan took this to be a smile. "Let's get back outside, and a younger man'll show you how it's done. . . . Come on, out the window."

The hand with the revolver gestured toward the open window, Nolan grabbed for the wrist and slammed the hand down against the wooden sill, once, and then again. On the third time fingers sprang open, and the gun dropped out the window. Nolan smashed his fist into the man's blackened temple, a blow with his whole body behind it. The hard little man crumpled and was out again.

Nolan leaned on the wall and gasped for breath. Half a minute went by and he was all right: his side was nagging him again, but he was all right.

He undid the watchdog's shirt collar and untied the tie, then used it to lash the man's slack wrists behind him and picked him up like a sack of grain and tossed him out the open window, where he landed in the hedge. Nolan figured he'd stay there a while longer this time around.

When he returned to the door to the study, Nolan peered in through the crack and saw Werner, undisturbed, still at his desk, reading. .38 in hand, Nolan drew back his foot and kicked the door open.

Werner dropped his book and sucked in air like a man going down for the third time. ". . . Nolan."

Nolan waved hello with the .38. He walked over to a chair in front of the desk, turned it backwards and sat down, looking at Werner straight on and leveling the .38 at him. . . .